SADDLE RIVER SPREAD

by

LYNN WESTLAND

An Abridged Edition of a $2.00
Western Thriller

Wildside Press

CHAPTER 1

IT WAS coming on for early dark, with a bank of black clouds swarming like clustering bees in the west, shutting away the last of the sun. A wind which had moaned before the dawn was still dolorous as it rustled the cured grass, and in the last hour it had taken on an added chill. The unpainted, one-room frame shack with its brave display of two glass windows, set in the little valley below, was already bright with the yellow splash of a coal-oil lamp, but Mrs. Hankins' single row of flowers, set against the side of the house, were wilted from an early frost.

The scene was a blending of hominess and the starkness of desolation, blank with the blight of poverty. But none of the riders, clustered ghostlike on the hilltop above, seemed to be moved by this or to feel the bravery or sense the pathetic wistfulness of struggle as embodied in those faded flowers. Wolf Masterson shifted his big hulk in the saddle, brows twitching together ominously.

"That's what I get for being soft," he growled. "First they squat, then they bring others of their breed to the country, like locusts. I was a fool to let them get a start."

The personal pronoun was heavy, emphatic, like the man himself. With Wolf Masterson it was always the personal. This was a part of his Wagon Wheel spread. He had come in here a quarter of a century before and had carved an empire, running his stock widely over open range. Long since, by that simple process of possession, he had come to believe implicitly that wherever his stock roamed, the land was his.

"They've got to go," he added sharply. "And I might as well make a beginnin' here as anywhere."

Two of the men stirred in the saddle, whether in uneasiness or hopeful expectancy would have been hard to say. Their faces betrayed nothing. The other man shook his head slowly.

That, too, was characteristic. Stumpy Garford was as big a man as Masterson, though but half his age. But where Masterson was impetuous, masterful, often rash, Stumpy was slow, quiet, though once determined on a course, there was no man in the Saddle River country who was more persistent in attaining to a desired end. His eyes were blue, al-

3

most dreamy, but his mouth was firm.

"Gloria is right friendly with Mis' Hankins," he suggested mildly.

"What if she is?" Masterson moved big shoulders impatiently. "She's always picking up stray dogs and cats and everything else of the same sort. And right now is no time for sentiment. It's got to the point where either these blasted nesters go, or we do. There's not room for all of us."

That was fact, and Stumpy agreed with him. The homesteaders were making a steady encroachment on the big cattle ranches, most of whose territory was still government land, and there was not going to be room for both to last very long. Already the first battles had gone to the nesters. But Stumpy did not agree with his employer that the way to win this battle was by terrorism or gun-play.

In the first exchange or so, that might work. But not for long. If one man was scared out, another would come who was made of sterner fibre. If he in turn was killed, a third would take his place, and the law, federal law, would be called in. And in such a case as that, it was the homesteaders who would have the law on their side.

A little child, a girl of perhaps three, had come to the cabin door, revealed in the splash of light from within. She stood framed there a moment, her hair softly golden and luminous, and Masterson growled deep in his throat and swung his horse about.

"With night comin' on, we won't bother them," he said, and rode for half a mile in silence, then pulled up abruptly again.

"Damn them anyway," he exploded. "I hate to fight women and children. But there's Radley and Tucker, and they haven't any womenfolks. Stumpy, come morning, you ride over and tell them it's open season on nesters. Tell them if they ain't out of here by sundown, it'll be sundown for them. That'll give the others a chance to get out without fighting."

Stumpy shook his head slowly.

"Radley might bluff," he said. "Tucker won't. And a lot of the others won't."

Masterson looked at him, gray eyes steely.

"If they want trouble, they can have all they want. You know how to use a gun, Stumpy."

That was true. Stumpy did know how to use a gun. Better,

probably, than any other man on the Wagon Wheel.

"It won't work," he said flatly. "It'll just mean war."

Masterson looked surprised. It wasn't often that any man, much less those who took his pay, ever disputed his opinions. But he was ready to make allowances for Stumpy Garford. There was no question but what Stumpy was a better man than most, in more ways than one. Likewise, it was easy to see that he was getting ideas about being Wolf Masterson's son-in-law, and if Masterson knew anything about women, Gloria rather liked the idea.

Not that Stumpy had said anything or given any outward indication that he counted on his position. But Masterson prided himself that he was no fool. In fact, if he had to have Gloria getting married, she could do a lot worse than pick this big cowboy. He was willing for to make allowances, but he wasn't willing for anybody, man, or devil, to seriously challenge his opinions or orders. That was why he was Wolf Masterson.

"If they want war, we'll give 'em a stomachfull," he pronounced.

Stumpy shook his head.

"You can, if you like," he agreed. "Not me."

Amazement ran across Masterson's face like a wind through grass, lifting the corners of his heavy mustache.

"Eh?" He jerked around in the saddle. "What did you say?"

"It won't work," Stumpy repeated. "They'll give us all the war we want, too—more than we can digest, likely. I'll tell them what you say, if you like, but I hired out as a cowboy, not as a gun-hand."

Scorn washed away the amazement in Masterson's steely eyes.

"Afraid of powder-smoke?" he taunted.

"Maybe," Stumpy admitted calmly. "Anyway, that's how it lays."

Masterson seemed about to say more, then abruptly he checked and put his horse into a gallop, the others following. His eyes narrowed calculatingly.

Riding behind him, Stumpy was not fooled. It wasn't like Wolf Masterson to hesitate, when he had anything to say or do. If he did, it was merely because he had a more crushing, devastating idea, and Stumpy had a pretty good notion what he had in mind now. Beneath the placid mask of his face, the cowboy's mind was troubled. It was taking an unfair advantage, hitting below the belt, to drag Gloria into this, but that, plainly enough, was what her father intended to do.

Having waited at all, he aimed to have the stage set to his own plan. Nothing was said as they pulled up at the big, comfortable log ranch house of the Wagon Wheel, or while the horses were being unsaddled and stabled. The early fall dark had come down on the ride home, the clouds had spread across the sky to blot out the hesitant stars, and Stumpy had an idea that there would be snow in the air before another dawn.

Summer was over, from all the signs. And in more ways than one. He had ridden up to this same ranch house one spring day, a year and a half before, and asked for a job. Receiving it, things had gone well for him since then—exceedingly well. Gloria had liked him—a lot, he was sure. So had her father. Things had been almost too good to last, and it didn't look as if they would last much longer.

There had been luck, in other ways—ways which no one on the Wagon Wheel, not even Gloria, knew anything about. Stumpy Garford had been a hard-working cowboy for half a dozen years before he had come to the Wagon Wheel. In those years he had saved close to a thousand dollars, which was more than unusual for a cowboy, and something that few of his acquaintances had even suspected.

But, in addition to that, he had, from time to time during those half-dozen years, taken some of his wages to grubstake an old friend who was down and out. Stumpy had never regretted the money. Baldy had been good to him when he was a friendless kid, and Baldy needed the money. Stumpy knew that the old prospector's bubbling enthusiasm that he would soon strike it rich was nothing new, and meant nothing. He had given him the money and never expected to see it again.

But the unexpected had happened, and he knew now that he was half-owner of a mine which, while not rich, was paying a handsome dividend on his investment. He could have mentioned this to Gloria and her father. But if she should be willing to marry him, one of these days, as he was, it would be a more pleasant surprise to find out that he wasn't exactly a penniless cowboy or a fortune-hunter.

Those eighteen months had been a long summer. But winter, from all the signs, was coming now. A flock of geese swept by, high overhead, honking mournfully. Winter. Well, he was ready for it.

Proof of Masterson's intentions was shown as he appeared to eat supper with the crew. Usually, Wolf dined in the big house with Gloria. Tonight he was coming out here to eat, and, of course at his suggestion, so was Gloria. The food was just as good—Masterson did not skimp his men—but he wouldn't be coming out tonight for nothing.

He was more jovial than was his wont during the meal, making no reference to the ride which the four of them had taken, until the meal was nearly at an end. Then he looked around the table.

"I've been figuring it up," he announced. "And there's thirteen squatters on Wagon Wheel land."

That, technically, wasn't correct. They were all homesteaders, and the land was government land, not Wagon Wheel, even though it had been included in Wagon Wheel range for a quarter of a century. But no one disputed his statement. Thirteen times a hundred and sixty meant roughly two thousand acres of land taken from the big ranch.

It was a big enough amount to be no longer insignificant, but the real significance lay in the fact that, if thirteen men had had the nerve to carve chunks out of the Wagon Wheel during the year, there would be many more of them the next season.

"Thirteen's going to be an unlucky number—a mighty unlucky number, for them," Masterson went on.

There were mutters of agreement. These men, most of them, had worked on the Wagon Wheel a long time. Men like Curly had come there when Gloria was a toddler, his own hair golden and wavy. Now it was silver, what there was of it, and the only curl that was left was above his ears and at the back of his neck. But to men who had spent the better part of a lifetime here, the Wagon Wheel meant almost as much as it did to Wolf Masterson himself.

Only Gloria looked troubled.

"But their families—" she protested.

"It's a case of self-preservation," Masterson said logically. "Either we get rid of them, or they'll take the ranch. I was in town today, and Fortymile's changing. It's swarming with new families, coming in, looking for land they can steal."

Gloria didn't argue. This thing had been coming for a long time, as certain and irrevocable as the winter itself, and she had seen and recognized it as well. She knew that, largely because of her, and her interest in the Hankins', who had been the first to come, her father had held off from any drastic action, hoping that the plague wouldn't develop to serious proportions.

"I put it up to Stumpy, here, to tell 'em to start movin', in the morning," her father went on. "He told me it'd mean war, and I said in that case we'd give it to 'em. But Stumpy won't fight."

He had thrown his bombshell, making it as climactic as he could. And in that gathering, with Gloria a guest for supper, it was sufficiently so. All eyes were suddenly upon Stumpy, Gloria's full of inquiry.

"I said it wouldn't work," Stumpy answered quietly. "It won't."

"If they want war, *I* said we'd give 'em plenty," Masterson repeated. His temper was rising again. "And I do the thinking here on the Wagon Wheel. Do you take orders—or are you afraid of the smell of powder-smoke?"

Stumpy Garford got slowly to his feet. It had come, at last. Winter. They thought, of course; they all thought, even Gloria, that he was afraid. And you couldn't explain—not to Wolf Masterson.

And to try and tell the others anything would be worse than useless. They were good cowboys, but mainly because they did as they were told, without thinking of the implications. Well, they'd have to think what they liked, including Gloria. He had mapped his own course, and he intended to follow it.

"Looks like we don't see eye to eye, Masterson," he said. "So, since I can't take your orders, I'll be ridin' in the morning."

CHAPTER 2

THERE WAS a skiff of snow on the ground in the morning, and a stiff east wind blowing, just as Stumpy had figured it the evening before. Clouds still hung low to the mournful horizon. A fitting day for leaving the Wagon Wheel. Wolf

Masterson had paid him, handing over the money frostily.

"In a way, I'm sorry to see you go, Garford," he said. Which was a rare confession for Wolf Masterson. "I'd had hopes of your amounting to something."

"I still have hopes," Stumpy said modestly, and let it go at that. His parting with Gloria was different. There was something close to tragedy in her eyes as she looked at him, and a redness, as though she had been crying.

"I don't understand, Stumpy," she said. Looking up at him, though she was an average-sized woman, she seemed little and frail. He had been nicknamed Stumpy as a boy of fourteen, when he had been small for his age. He wasn't small now, but he felt so in that moment.

"It's kind of hard to explain, Gloria," he said slowly. "But seems like your dad and I just don't see alike. So it'll be better this way."

"But you could still have stayed—you didn't have to quit, just because of what he said—"

"I reckon I'd of been quitting pretty soon, anyway—whether this had come up or not," he said gently.

She looked at him in surprise, not understanding.

"But what are you going to do?" she asked. "If you leave the country—" The unvoiced words carried a deeper meaning than she would have trusted herself to speak.

"I won't be leaving the country," Stumpy explained. "I'll not be very far off—not if you want to see me any time, or need me. Fact is, I'm kind of aimin' to set up in business for myself."

He didn't elaborate on that, and, having come to know him pretty well, Gloria didn't ask. When he felt that the time had come to explain his meaning, he'd do it, but not before. But there was an odd sense of comfort in the news that he wasn't going far away.

"I still wish you could stay here," she said simply.

"So do I," he agreed. "It would be a lot easier. But seems like the things that amount to anything aren't easy. If you need help, any time—you come to me, or send me word."

"I'll come, Stumpy," she promised. Neither of them said any more. Both knew that, with shadows hovering, it wasn't the time or place.

He was stopped once more before he had quit the wide borders of the Wagon Wheel. Chinook, a sandy-haired young puncher who had come to the Wagon Wheel not long after himself, came riding up to say so-long. The others of the crew, plainly disappointed in him, hadn't bothered with that formality.

"Ridin' far, Stumpy?" he asked.

Stumpy shook his head.

"Thought I'd head up North of Saddle River," he explained.

Chinook grinned.

"Wait while I go draw my pay," he said. "I'll ride along. Things are getting too gosh-durn quiet down here for my taste."

"From the looks, they'll be hottin' up some, right soon."

"Maybe. See here, Stumpy," Chinook exploded. "I've rode circle with you a good many times, slept in the same blankets with you. Some of the boys are fool enough to figger that you're headin' out because there's a fight shapin' up, and they think same's the old man, that you're scared. I know a damn sight better."

"Well, I ain't right partial to getting in a scrap that can come out only one way," Stumpy confessed.

"Maybe, but you ain't scared. These nesters are getting to be a problem."

"Yeah. The biggest one since the Indians was chased off to reservations."

"Well, wait, like I say, and I'll go draw my pay."

"No hurry, Chinook. I'll be around Fortymile two-three days. And if I go North of the river, I won't be askin' for a job, punchin' cows."

Chinook studied him a moment, eyes narrowed. Like Gloria, he knew better than to ask him what he had in mind, until Stumpy was in a mood to tell. But that last sentence was revealing.

Here, twenty miles to the south of Saddle River, Wolf Masterson and his Wagon Wheel had long been the big spread. There were lesser spreads to the south of the river, however, and a considerable scattering of homesteaders in the last few months. South of Saddle River was, in a broad way of speaking, civilized country.

North of the river was a different proposition. There was just one spread to the north, and that was Mart Cloud's Longhorn Ranch. If Wolf Masterson was a big man on this side, Mart Cloud was a bigger man on that side.

He had long had a habit of making his own laws, as inflexible as those of the Medes and Persians. He had let it be known that the land North of Saddle River was a part of the Longhorn range, and that he would brook no interference from anyone. There had been occasions in the past when men had tried to challenge his edict, among them powerful cattlemen seeking more pasture. The law had been clarified and confirmed in gun-smoke. For a long time there had been no further challenge.

So well known was the rule now, that no homesteaders had tried to move north of the river. That was Longhorn country. And now, if Stumpy Garford said that he was going north of the river, but not to ask for a job punching cows—there was something in the wind.

"And them misguided hombres are thinkin' you're quittin' here because you're afraid of trouble," Chinook grinned. "Reckon I'll be joinin' you in two-three days. Providin' you won't think I'm in the way."

"If that's the way you feel, I'll be needin' me a foreman," Stumpy nodded, and headed on down the road.

He was stopped once again before reaching Fortymile. This time by a caravan of wagons heading out from town, toward the Wagon Wheel. Three wagons, two of them decrepit-looking outfits pulled by sorry teams. The other was newer, bigger, with a spanking team of white horses. All three were piled high with household goods, plows, miscellaneous gear—homestead stuff.

The driver of the newer wagon, who was in the lead, hailed him peremptorily, pulling up. He was a big man, square built all the way up, with stiff black hair which jutted up like a porcupine's quills, and a stubble of black beard, all of which gave him a decided resemblance to a grizzly bear.

"This the way to the Wagon Wheel?" he demanded, and his voice was heavy, truculent.

Stumpy nodded, with an instant feeling that he didn't like this man.

"That's it."

"Plenty good land out there, I hear?"

"Plenty. But it ain't cheap land."

"What do you mean, not cheap land?"

"Any that get it'll have to pay for it—in blood and bullets."

The square-built man threw back his head and roared with laughter, though the drivers of the following wagons looked scared at the news.

"The Wagon Wheel don't fight," he proclaimed.

"Startin' today, Masterson aims to put up a scrap," Stumpy amplified.

"Oh, he does, eh? Well, if it's trouble he's lookin' for, he'll get a bellyfull. You can tell him Tom Bannack, from Dakota, said so." He clucked to his horses and the wagon jolted forward again. After a momentary hesitation, the others followed.

Stumpy watched them rumble ahead, eyes narrowed. It looked as if showdown was a lot closer for the Wagon Wheel than he had figured, even. Not that three more homesteaders, in themselves, would make much difference. But the original thirteen had lacked a leader. Wolf Masterson might get away with his bluff, for a time. But Stumpy had a hunch that they were about to get a leader. And given leadership, they would fight.

He hesitated momentarily. If there was going to be real trouble back there, with Gloria in the middle of it—then he shrugged and rode on. It wouldn't be that bad. And the thing that he had foreseen was here. Something bigger than any single man or group of men, a force as inexorable as those other waves which had flowed successively across a continent, breaking occasionally like waves on a rocky shore, but swept farther and farther by successive waves which kept coming from behind.

First it had been the fur traders and trappers, the explorers. Then the vanguard of homeseekers, till the prairies were crossed and they had run up against the mountains. There a new movement had taken form.

With the first influx of land-hungry men spreading over half a continent, it had taken them a while to assimilate such a huge bite, and this wilder country had been left, for a season, to the cattlemen. Crowded out of Kansas and Nebraska and the great prairie states, they had found sanctuary here, pushing back the Indians, carving out huge empires for themselves in the free land.

To some of them it had seemed that they were so remote from the last fringes of civilization that they were forever safe from encroachment. Towns had been a hundred miles apart, cities a thousand. Wolf Masterson was a man who had believed that his was an empire which could have no end, at least in his lifetime. Mart Cloud, North of Saddle River, was another.

But now the slack had been taken up, the land to the south and east was taken, old settled country, and a new generation, with the same hot blood of foot-itching ancestors in their veins, were pushing on, looking in their turn for new frontiers, for free land. Already they had come, like the locusts. Wave after wave had swept across a continent, each new wave making drastic changes. And you couldn't stop the ocean, nor could you check these waves of men.

But there was more than one way of skinning a cat.

CHAPTER 3

BEFORE HE had been half a day in Fortymile, Stumpy knew that the story of his leaving the Wagon Wheel had reached town as well. It was an amazing thing how news could travel so fast, but he had long since ceased to marvel at it.

Now he knew, from the way men looked at him, what they were saying. That he had quit his job because he was afraid of a fight which seemed to be on the way.

He was quietly busy for the next couple of days, until Chinook rode into town and hunted him up. Even then, Stumpy was no more communicative.

"Things look right promisin', Chinook," he said. "Come morning, I'm taking a little trip up north of the river, just to look around. You stay in town till I get back, and kind of take yourself a vacation. You'll need it. And you can be laying in a few supplies. Here's a list and some money."

He handed Chinook the entire sum which Wolf Masterson had paid him in wages, and there had been a lot of back pay coming when he had quit the Wagon Wheel. Chinook whistled.

"You aimin' to equip an army?" he asked.

"Not exactly," Stumpy denied. "But there's nothing like being ready. Do things kind of on the quiet."

"Sure. You're not afraid to trust me with this much money? I might be in some other country, time you come back here."

"If you did, I figure you'd be the big loser," Stumpy said, and dismissed the matter. "Any trouble on the Wagon Wheel yet?"

"Not much, so far," Chinook confessed. "Wolf, he passed the word around that the nesters had to get clear off the borders of the ranch or they'd be cleared out, but he got soft-hearted and gave 'em a week to do it in."

That, Stumpy reflected, had all the earmarks of being a bad mistake. In a week, Bannack could have the homesteaders organized for a fight, and with a motive like this, they probably would. But it was Masterson's affair, and, proud old Longhorn that he was, he'd run it his way regardless.

It was mid-afternoon of the next day when Stumpy crossed to the north of Saddle River. It was a wide, turgid stream here, a gleaming silver barrier in the sun. Gently rising hills, partly timbered, rose beyond it, and on the southern bank was a sheltered expanse with more timber behind. The ford was not a difficult one, but it was the only good crossing for miles up or down the river.

The snow of a few days had melted, and the weather now held promise of a few nice weeks before winter should set in in earnest.

Few people, aside from the Longhorn crew, ever crossed Saddle River. Many had looked longingly toward the land which lay to the north, but most of them had heeded the warnings which had been so potently enforced in the past. Here was knee-high grass, brown and cured and succulent, untouched at all during the long summer. It was a big range —a vast country which Mart Cloud had taken for himself.

Stumpy viewed it with increasing interest. He had never been up this way before, though he had talked with men who had, and so had a pretty good idea of what it was like. There was a side-stream, the so-called Dry Fork of Saddle River, which came down from the north, and this Dry Fork divided the country up here naturally into two empiric divisions, east and west, both of them comprising some of the finest land which ever lay outdoors.

The buildings and headquarters of the Longhorn were off to the west of the Dry Fork, so Stumpy did not bother to go near them. He rode around for the rest of the afternoon without encountering either a steer, horse or man, or any recent sign of them, which was proof enough of the bigness of this territory which Mart Cloud claimed for his own.

As evening came on, Stumpy made his camp in a little wooded glade, hobbling his horse and spreading his blankets in a vast content. He helped himself to trout from a small stream which ran to join the Dry Fork, and added them to a few slices of bacon, with biscuits browned between two pans. He was lying on his back, contemplating the stars as they pricked out the sky in an increasing pattern of stretching infinity, when hoofbeats sounded and two men rode up to his camp fire.

Stumpy sat up and regarded them, recognizing Mart Cloud instantly. He had seen the boss of the Longhorn a few months back, and once seen, Mart Cloud was not easily forgotten. Like Wolf Masterson, there was a dominance about him which stamped itself forcefully upon men and events. He too, was big—tall, slender-seeming, but bewilderingly powerful, handsome, and surprisingly young for a man who had dominated the country North of Saddle River until he had become almost a legend.

"Saw your smoke, and thought we'd have a look," he greeted, swinging down from the saddle. He hunkered down, rolling a quirly expertly, his eyes taking in every detail of the man and the night camp. "Haven't I seen you before?" he challenged.

"Yeah," Stumpy admitted. "I was with Wolf Masterson at the roundup, last spring. Some of your stock had swum the river."

"I remember now," Cloud nodded. "You're Garford— Stumpy Garford. There's no Wagon Wheel stuff up this way."

It was a natural error to fall into, that Stumpy should be scouring the country for strays. But he corrected it.

"I'm not with the Wagon Wheel any longer."

"No? Lookin' for a job up this way? I can use a good man."

"I've kind of got me a job. Though I do like it up this way." Stumpy sat up a little straighter. "Cloud, I'd like to buy me some land, right in here. Nice country."

Cloud laughed good-naturedly.

"It is nice country. But I'm keepin' it from being broken up. No can do."

"I know how you feel. But you can't keep on holdin' it

forever, Cloud. Times are changin'."

Cloud bristled.

"Who says I can't?" he challenged.

"It stands to reason. This is good country—mighty good country. And you see what's been happening to the Wagon Wheel already. I'd sure like to do business with you, Cloud."

Cloud seemed undecided whether to be angry or amused. He chose the latter.

"How much land would you like?" he asked, as if to humor a small child.

"Well, I've been kind of looking around. Your headquarters are over to the west, the other side of the Fork. There's as big a country there as one man can ever hope to use. Over this side, to the east, right in here, there's a section of maybe eight thousand acres, all together, mighty fine land. I'd like it a lot."

"And what would you give me for it?"

"Ten thousand."

Cloud stared, a little surprised.

"Cash, I suppose?" he asked, and was amused again.

"Cash," Stumpy agreed.

Cloud laughed and got to his feet.

"I kind of like you, Stumpy," he conceded. "You've got a sense of humor. But I'm holdin' the country North of Saddle River—all of it. Come hell or high water."

"Well, I don't know's I blame you," Stumpy agreed. "Though you're makin' the same mistake as Masterson, way it looks to me. Sorry we can't do business."

*   *   *

There was news in Fortymile, the next afternoon. News which was another straw in the wind. Old Man Proctor, who had run the B in a Box ranch for thirty years, had finally quit. His ranch, a big one a couple of years before, had lain south and east of the Wagon Wheel. In the very nature of things, the homesteaders had reached there first.

Like Wolf Masterson, Proctor had been inclined to temporize at first, slow to recognize the danger. Besides, he had had his share of trouble in his younger days, and had declared more than once that all he wanted now was to be left alone, to run his herds and spend his declining days in peace. Which had been a vain hope.

Alarmed at last, he had determined to fight. There had been some powder burnt and considerable trouble, and the rest of the country had watched with tense interest. Even up to a few days ago, the issue had hung in the balance.

But now Old Man Proctor and the B had lost their sting. He had made an agreement with the nesters, letting them have what was left without a fight, in return for a small payment per acre. That payment, on their part, had been partly generosity, because most of them secretly rather liked and admired and had been sorry for the old-timer, and partly it had been a good business proposition, to save further trouble. For the land which he had claimed for so long was all government land, open under the law to homesteaders, and legally they did not need to pay him anything.

Now it was settled. The B in a Box herds had been sold, and with all the proceeds, Old Man Proctor was well fixed, able to leave the country for a more temperate clime as winter came on, to spend his last days in the peace he craved. But it was a victory which would speedily bring in fresh swarms of nesters to the entire country.

Fortymile was buzzing with it. Doubly so, because Proctor's entire crew of some thirty men had arrived in a bunch, out of work, though with a generous bonus added to their wages, and unsure what to do now in a changing world. Chinook brought the news to Stumpy as he returned to town.

Stumpy beamed.

"That's luck, for us," he said. "I know those boys—good ones, every one of them. Go right down and hire them, first thing, Chinook, at regular puncher's wages. I got a little work to tend to this afternoon, but I'll meet you and the boys outside of town, at the camp ground, come dark. Have them there, and those supplies you've been buyin', loaded in wagons."

"Sure," agreed Chinook. "And where do we go with that crew and all that stuff?"

"Come morning," said Stumpy, "we move North of Saddle River."

CHAPTER 4

THE LITTLE business, which Stumpy had had to attend to, had kept him busy for a considerable length of time, and had occasioned more than passing amazement in certain quarters of Fortymile, though the men who had handled that business had long since believed themselves immune to anything which might happen in this rapidly changing world.

But it had been attended to in a manner satisfactory to all concerned at that end of the line, and Stumpy had arrived at the rendezvous half an hour after dark-fall, accompanied by a dozen more men. He had scoured the town to find them, but he had been choosy in his picking. Ordinary men wouldn't do.

The camp ground, some three miles from town, was a patch of several open acres down by the road, where Beaver Creek crossed it. Cattlemen were accustomed to stop there to feed and water, and others often camped overnight, especially when making a two-day journey to town and back.

Chinook whistled as Stumpy rode in with the additional recruits.

"What is this, an army?" he demanded. "I can't quite figger it, Stumpy."

"We're going North of Saddle River," Stumpy explained. "There'll be trouble—but we've got just about a big enough crew to handle it. If any of you don't like the job, of course, you don't have to go along."

There was a moment of silence, broken by a laugh.

"And they was tellin' around town that yuh quit at the Wagon Wheel 'cause yuh was afraid of trouble."

That was that. Stumpy grinned back at them.

"Just one more thing," he said. "I'm payin' you regular wages, and I'm askin' two things. The first is that you let me run this show, and do as I say, all the way through. It'll be within the law, don't worry about that none. What I want is loyalty, same as anywhere else, and I know I'll get it. You're takin' my wages to do as I say. The second, is that you stick till the job's done."

"If you can pay the wages, Stumpy, we'll stick," someone yelled back.

"You'll get your wages," Stumpy agreed.

Knowing him, they knew that he meant exactly what he said, and they were satisfied.

"I s'pose you're aimin' to get you a big ranch up there?" Chinook asked.

"That's my idea," Stumpy agreed.

"What you going to do with it, if I'm not too curious? You got any herd?"

Stumpy's eyes clouded a little.

"I'm hopin' to get it ready in time for the herd," he said ambiguously.

Still not at all sure what their employer really had in mind, they went with him the next day, crossing Saddle River again shortly after noon. By mid-afternoon, riding a little ahead of the others, Stumpy had reached the spot where he had camped a couple of nights before.

He had liked the spot on sight. There was a little hill for shelter, the creek winding by, a fine spring bubbling out of the hill and running to join it. There was a grove of cotton-woods, and clumps of service-berry, dogwood, choke-cherry and other brush close by. It would be an ideal place for building a home.

He wasn't surprised when, almost as he reached it, Mart Cloud rode into sight from the opposite direction, with half a dozen men behind him. Today there was no welcoming smile on the cattleman's face. At least some of the trespassers had been sighted from a distance, of course, and Cloud lost no time in coming to investigate.

"So you're back, eh, Garford?" he snapped. "This your party?"

"Reckon so," Stumpy conceded.

The wagons and the men who rode with them were still out of sight. He doubted if Mart Cloud had any very clear idea yet as to the magnitude of this invasion.

"Well," said Cloud, deliberately. "You can turn around and get straight back across the river. And don't come this way again."

Stumpy shook his head.

"Sorry, Cloud. I can't do that."

"No?" Cloud's brows twitched together like piling thunder-heads. "What the devil do you want here, anyway?"

"Land," said Stumpy softly. "Same as I told you the other day, Cloud. But I'm not lookin' for trouble. I—"

Cloud's laugh was not pleasant. He waved one hand to the men grouped behind him.

"If you stay here, that's what you'll get. Plenty!"

"Like I was sayin', Cloud, I'd rather not have trouble.

I'm still willing to give you ten thousand, cash, for this land in here."

"And I'm tellin' you to go to the devil."

"It comes down to this," Stumpy went on. "You can't hold this land. Not for long. So I figure it might as well be me as anybody, to have it. But I'd like to be neighborly."

"You've got a gall," Cloud said hotly. "And nobody takes a foot of my land. Do you start travelin' now, or do I plant you right here?"

One of Cloud's men gave a startled ejaculation. Cloud swung, and following his gaze, stared in growing amazement. The riders had swung into sight now, coming two and two, a long line of them, then the laden wagons in the middle of the cavalcade, and more horsemen behind them. Cloud's jaw dropped a little at the number of them. Then he swung back angrily.

"Are these your men? What the devil's the idea?"

"They're my men," Stumpy agreed. "Forty-four in all, countin' myself. There'll be a half-dozen more in a few days."

"And do you think—" Cloud was almost choking in his wrath. "Do you think that you can bluff me—that you can come in here and steal this land right out from under my nose?"

"I'm not tryin' to bluff you, Cloud." Stumpy's own men were close enough now to hear—to listen to the first explanation he had given to any of them. "As to stealin' this land, you're a mite off the track. This whole section in here—about eight thousand acres, all layin' in one big chunk together, has been homesteaded, by myself and my men. It was open, government land, and we filed on it. It belongs to us, and the government's back of us. If you try to interfere, you're going against the federal government. Chew on that."

Cloud spluttered for a moment in impotent, helpless rage. Here was the menace which had shadowed the country for a year and more, the thing which had licked Old Man Proctor and was beating a lot of others. He had laughed at it, but he had counted on homesteaders coming in a small trickle, as they had done in other places. More than that, he had figured on having to deal with tenderfeet, not with cowboys of the stamp of Stumpy Garford. The thing was staggering.

"Why, you—you damned thief—" he gasped.

"Take it easy," Stumpy suggested. "We're here, Cloud,

and don't make any mistake about it, we're stayin' here. But I'm doing you a favor, if you only knew it. I'm takin' land in one big chunk, instead of a lot of scattered homesteads, and all east of the Dry Fork. Which still leaves you your land to the west. And in lookin' it up, down at the court house, I found it was worse than I'd suspected. You're like all the other old-timers—a damn sight bigger fool than I thought could run at large."

"What the blazes do you mean?" Cloud growled.

"You don't own a foot of the land you've been claimin' for your own all these years. Not a foot. I'd have thought that you'd of had sense enough to file on a hundred and sixty in your own name, at least. You can call it chicken feed, but it'd protect your buildings and give you a little legal right in the country. But it's not too late. Get busy and file, and have your men do the same. You can save a big ranch, west of the Fork, and have it as long as the sun shines on it."

It was, plainly, a new idea to Cloud, as it was to all the cattlemen and old-timers in the country, that they might beat the homesteaders by using their own weapon, to protect themselves. But if Cloud was grateful for the suggestion, his face did not show it.

"You've got forty-four men here, eh?" he grated. "Well, let me tell you something. Land that's homesteaded is only yours if you live on it three years, and you'll all be damned lucky if you're alive three days from now—unless you skedaddle back south across the river in a hurry. I've got a big crew, and I'll not stand for any—"

His language, at that point, grew lurid and descriptive. Stumpy's face reddened, and he swung down from the saddle.

"Shut up!" he said, and his voice, quiet as it was, carried above the frenzy of Cloud's. "This is my land, and no man talks to me that way on my land. Get off it—or get off your horse!"

Cloud stared for a moment, amazed. Then, bellowing, he was off his horse and rushing. Like all the rest, it was a tradition in the country that Mart Cloud could lick any man who came along, either with fists or guns.

CHAPTER 5

STUMPY WASN'T afraid of tradition, but Mart Cloud was a different proposition, and he had no delusions as to the size of the job he had taken on now. Battling him for a ranch here North of Saddle River was a man's-sized job in itself. A fist fight loomed even bigger, and he would have preferred to have that postponed awhile.

Not that he was afraid of Cloud, either, or of taking a licking. He could do that, if he had to. The trouble, right now, was that he was in the position of an interloper in this game he was playing. He had hired a lot of men, who were challenged by the daring and bigness of the proposition he had put up to them, and because of that they were willing to go along with him, to follow him to hell and back—so long as he led the way.

That was where the catch came in. To keep them following, he had to keep leading. Up to a day or so before, he had been one of them, just another cowboy, well enough liked by most of them. But that had been all. There had been speculation as to whether he would become son-in-law to Wolf Masterson and, by that route, become in time boss of the Wagon Wheel and a full-fledged cattleman.

He hadn't waited for that devious route, but had jumped ahead on his own hook. In challenging Mart Cloud, he had set himself up to be a cattleman, but he had to make good on that brash assumption.

It was that knowledge, that he was being weighed by his own men as well as by Mart Cloud, that drove him forward now. He met Cloud's rush squarely, taking a glancing blow by ducking under it, allowing it to slide over his shoulder and past his ear. It had all the driving viciousness of a grizzly's paw, and if it had landed squarely, would have been just about as devastating.

But he landed a straight right and a jabbing left to jaw and nose as he came up under it, stopping Cloud's rush and standing him back on his heels. Only for a moment, however. He could see by the sudden wariness of Cloud's eyes that he was surprised, but that was all. Without warning Cloud jerked up a knee at close quarters, a treacherous blow aimed to catch Stumpy in the groin and disable him.

Stumpy saw the knee coming. He twisted, reaching down,

grabbed the leg and, putting all his body into the effort, started to swing. Caught off guard, Cloud suddenly found himself on his back, leg up in the air, then, as Stumpy's swing really got started, he was jerked into motion like the rim of a wheel, with his leg for the spoke and Stumpy for the hub.

It was a devastating trick if it could be worked, and, sweat breaking from his face with the effort, Stumpy was working it. Cloud was clear off the ground, now. Once, twice, Stumpy turned, swinging him in a complete circle, faster and faster, body gradually rising higher. At the apex of his swing he let go, and Cloud shot away for twenty feet, landing on his back with a jarring thud.

A gasp went up from the onlookers. They had seen the flash of that knee, had expected to see Stumpy on the ground a moment later, writhing in pain, the fight all but over. The swift turn had caught them as unprepared as it had Cloud.

But Mart Cloud had not acquired his reputation as a king North of Saddle River, or as a tough fighter, without good cause. For an instant he lay prone. Only an instant. The next moment, a little groggily but determined, he was coming to his feet, wading back for more.

There was plenty more of it in the next few minutes. Give and take, slugging it out, a battle of giants. A hush had fallen on the ring of spectators. This sort of thing couldn't last long, not at that pace. After what had happened already, it was anybody's battle.

There was the salty taste of blood in his mouth, his lips were cut and bleeding, one sleeve torn nearly off his shirt, red welts making themselves seen and felt over his face and the upper part of his body. Stumpy was taking a lot of punishment, and he knew it.

Only two things kept him going. The knowledge that this was the testing time, the battle that would win or lose, whatever might happen later on, if he won this one. He could win it and lose in the end, but if he lost it now there could be no others to follow. He had to win.

The other factor was the knowledge that Mart Cloud was as bad off as he was. If he looked like a fresh-pounded beefsteak, Cloud looked no better, and there was the same groggy stare in his eyes, his blows were losing that vicious sting. Just a little more—

Stumpy leaned forward, putting all that remained of his

strength into a straight left to the jaw. He knew that Cloud saw it coming, but he couldn't dodge it. Somehow he did strike back at the same moment, then he was going down— flat on his back again.

Weaving, Stumpy stood over him, staring glassy-eyed, shaking his head, trying to clear it. But that last haymaker of Cloud's had been just about as bad as his own, and he couldn't shake off the effects of it. He felt his knees buckling, but he didn't go down—not on top of Cloud.

For in the king of Saddle River there was an unexpected reserve of strength which, surprisingly enough, he brought now into sudden, vicious play. His legs drew back, then, as Stumpy started to fall, he had lifted them like pistons. His feet caught Stumpy in the chest, hurtling him back for a dozen feet to fall in a heap, the jar of it taking all the breath that was left in him.

Gasping, dazed, the world reeling about him, Stumpy was aware that Cloud had gotten to his feet, was advancing grimly upon him. A kind of paralysis gripped Stumpy. He knew what Cloud intended to do—to jump at him, coming down on him with both booted feet, to finish him in a bone-crushing finale which could admit of no argument. Desperately he twisted a little, rolled as Cloud jumped. His arms reached out, wrapped themselves around Cloud's ankles, and the next moment he had brought Cloud crashing down as well.

His breath was coming back now. Stumpy gained his feet, warily. But the fight was over. In falling, Cloud's head had hit a stone, and he was out cold.

Men were talking again, low-toned with the amazement of it. Cloud stirred, sat up, and looked dazedly about. He dragged himself to his feet, his eyes black, walked across to his horse. Then he turned.

"You were lucky, this time," he blazed suddenly. "But this ain't the end, Garford—it's only the beginning. And I'll run you off this range if it's the last thing I do."

Silently then, his men behind him, he rode away. But his going was a little marred by the grins on the faces of Stumpy's crew. Seeing them, Stumpy forgot the pain of bruised flesh. After this, whatever else might happen, he had them behind him, their loyalty a sure thing. By that battle, he had proven his right to be a cattleman.

For the next few days they were left to work unmolested.

There was a house to be built, bunkhouse, barns and corral—the beginnings of a new outfit, the Saddle. With eight thousand acres or so in here, a man could have a nice herd of cattle and do right well.

Stumpy was dreaming as he looked around the little valley which he had chosen for home. Eight thousand acres, these days, wasn't much—not to men like Wolf Masterson or Mart Cloud, men who had simply taken empires out of unending miles of free land and then had been able to ride for hours or even days across land which they called their own. Only it hadn't been their own. That was the catch.

To them, in their heyday, the idea of eight or ten thousand acres comprising a ranch would cause a snort of derision. But as compared to a hundred and sixty, the quarter-sections which the nesters were grabbing from these unfenced empires, it was a lot. And it stacked up mighty well now alongside the vanishing acres of men like Old Man Proctor. Soon it would look big to men like Masterson and Cloud.

Not that Stumpy, in his dreams, was content with that much territory. He was looking a long way ahead. The nesters would continue to swarm in, overrunning the country like a swarm of locusts, breaking the primeval sod with the plow, changing a country—ruining a country, in his opinion. That sort of thing was all right in some places, but it wouldn't work here—not for long.   ·

There was pretty fair soil through this whole country, and for a few years, he judged, the homesteaders would get pretty fair crops off it, enjoying a few years of false prosperity. But those years wouldn't last, and with eight thousand acres he could afford to wait for the grim aftermath.

That it would come too, he was as certain as that the nesters were here now. For in this country, you couldn't count on rain for crops, not more than one year out of three. The other two years, on an average, rainfall was something hoped for but pretty much done without. In those dry years, wheat and crops that depended on the plow and rain would be pretty much of a failure. And a few lean years would discourage a lot of nesters.

After that, if a man was established, you could buy up their holdings pretty cheap, seed the torn lands down to pasture again, and run cattle. Grass would grow with a lot less rain than wheat. Hot weather might shrivel it in mid-

summer, but if it had grown, the crop was there, and a few
dry days couldn't ruin a season, nor a hail storm wipe a
year's toil away.

He turned back to realities. That would come, but only if
he made a go of it now. This was a battle for existence, and
only the strong and far-seeing would be here to take advantage of the breaks which must come later on. Wolf Masterson and Old Man Proctor had been strong, but not far-
seeing. He aimed to be both.

"We'll build a house and barn and corrals right here," he
said. "The lumber will start coming along pretty soon, but
we'll use that for homestead shacks. These main buildings
will be of logs. Did you bring saws and axes, Chinook?"

Chinook nodded.

"Right here." He looked speculatively at a hillside covered
with tall, straight pines. "Some good logs there, all right—
if we can handle 'em."

"We'll handle them all right," Stumpy said confidently.
"You boys who like an axe can start in with them, the others
can use the saws. I'll take an axe."

He picked up a keen, broad-bitted axe and started for the
trees. A little dubiously, the others made their selections and
followed him.

Stumpy selected a tree and set to work. The others were
doing the same, but, grinning to himself, Stumpy could tell
the difference. His own tree was being cut as cleanly as with
a saw, each stroke of the axe sinking deeply, one following
the other exactly. That was something which he had learned
from a year in the lumber woods. At the time, a cowboy at
heart, he hadn't relished the job, but some of its teachings
were handy now.

The tree wavered, swayed, and crashed down. Chinook
eyed it with admiration mixed with awe.

"How do yuh do it?" he demanded. "Mine looks like it'd
been chewed on some, but all I've got, so far, is a blister."

From off at one side, along with the uneasy whine of a
saw, came the rather bitter plaint of a bald-headed old-timer
appropriately named Onion.

"Red," he adjured his more youthful pardner, "I don't
partic'ly mind havin' tuh drag the saw my way and push
it back to yuh ag'in—I used tuh do that years ago. But if
yuh want a ride, how about saddlin' yore cayuse? Be more

comfortable for both of us, than ridin' on the saw."

But in the next day or so the work was going forward. Logs were felled, peeled, notched, lifted into place. Now the chuck wagon was in place under a tree, the cook busily at work there, but there would soon be a house here, a cook shack there. It was all much the same as with a round-up crew, except that there was no herd to watch. The herd would come later—and not much later, Stumpy had a hunch. He only hoped that he could have the range ready by the time the cattle would need it.

Then, on the third day following their arrival north of the river, the men hauling in supplies from town brought news. There had been a big gun battle on the Wagon Wheel—a battle for possession of the ranch, between nesters and cowboys.

Apparently the fight had been indecisive. But men had been shot on both sides, some seriously, and from an acrimonious bickering the feud had suddenly become tense and bitter. Now there was blood on the moon, and it would soon be spilling over.

CHAPTER 6

THOUGH HE had been expecting news of just about that sort from the Wagon Wheel, the actual receipt of it was disturbing, none the less. Gloria was there, and, knowing her, Stumpy knew that she would be in the thick of trouble in more ways than one. But the news only caused him to intensify his preparations on the Saddle.

With the regular buildings well started, he turned his attention to the claim shacks. Lumber was coming in on his wagons every day, being hauled from Fortymile, the drivers escorted from the river by several armed men. The claim shacks were an essential part of the whole program.

"We'll build a couple dozen of them," he instructed Chinook. "Build them here, six feet wide and fourteen long, set on wooden runners. Then we can pull them to the claims. They'll slide along easy on the grass, especially when we get a little snow."

Chinook nodded.

"Sure. But why two dozen? We'll have twice that many claims."

"And a shack will set on the line across two homesteads, half on each side," Stumpy pointed out. "That way, each man can sleep on his own land, but there'll be two men together in each house."

"Mighty good idea," Chinook conceded. "One man alone is a pretty dangerous proposition, but two together can put up a scrap, if so be it's needed. And I've a hunch there'll be trouble castin' a wide loop over this range yet."

"Sort of figured so, myself," Stumpy agreed.

He was pleased to see that his crew took this part of it as a matter of course. Almost without exception they had been cowboys, trained in the cattleman's tradition, and as such they had looked askance at the nesters crowding into the cow country. Now they were filing on homesteads themselves. But taking a big block of land to form one big ranch took most of the sting from the proceeding, as they viewed it.

What was equally to the point, they accepted without question the ethics of the thing. It would be their job to live on this land, as homesteaders, to "prove up" on their quartersections and receive title, then to turn the land over to Stumpy for a small premium above their regular wages. He was paying them wages for doing that, and it was all a part of the job. Somebody had to have the land. They knew that it was better suited to cattle than to wheat, and they preferred to see it kept for cattle.

The surveyors arrived the next day, with their chains and instruments, ready to run the lines of the various homesteads—the first men of their calling ever to set foot North of Saddle River.

Exultation grew in Stumpy as he walked over the land. He had known from the first that it was fine country; there was fine pasture, good water, excellent shelter. And it was his.

His, so long as he could hold it. No longer. Cloud had held it a long time, and his fingers were eager to grasp it again. Nor were his the only greedy fingers. Wars had been fought for empires, and would be again. And this was empire.

Someone was coming. Absorbed in his calculations, assuming it to be one of the surveyors, Stumpy did not immediately look up. When he finally turned, a chill wind seemed to lift the short hairs at the base of his scalp. It was Mart Cloud riding toward him, and not a hundred feet away.

Cloud's eyes were fixed on him, sharply, unpleasantly, quick to note the absence of Stumpy's belt and gun today. His horse continued to approach at a walk, and a mocking smile twisted Cloud's mouth. With unhurried deliberation, never taking his eyes off Stumpy, he reached, found the strap and gave a jerk to the knot which loosened his coiled lariat, near the front of the saddle. Then he started to shake out the loop.

"I warned you, Garford, that I'd run you off this place," Cloud said. "You had your chance to start makin' tracks— and didn't take it. So this is it."

His voice was chill as a winter blizzard, and he had the coil of rope shaken out now, the loop beginning to swing a little with the practiced ease of a man much used to it. Stumpy watched him warily. No need to ask what Cloud had in mind, for he knew only too well.

It was Cloud's intention to rope him—getting that noose around his neck, turning his horse in a quick gallop to jerk it tight, pulling Stumpy off his feet at the same time. After that, there wouldn't be much more to it. A few minutes of dragging him would be enough, even if the initial jerk didn't break his neck.

Stumpy had started to retreat, backing warily, keeping his eyes on Cloud. The cattleman wasn't hurrying any. There was plenty of time, and he knew it. By now he was convinced that Stumpy had no gun on him. And if he missed the first throw, or even the first ten, there was still plenty of time.

And, if Stumpy proved too hard to rope, Cloud always had his gun as a last resort. But he didn't figure to need it. Shooting down an unarmed man was something that would be frowned on, even on this side of the river. But the rope, for a nester, was different.

Stumpy was under no illusions as to his chances. A man could catch a running steer by one foot, or do a lot of other fancy things with a rope, if he knew how. Such as settling the loop over one pair of horns in a close-packed herd of milling cattle. All of that was just about as difficult as what Cloud figured to do now.

The rope shot out suddenly, coming with almost the speed and precision of a striking snake. Stumpy threw up his arm, but he wasn't trying to fend the loop off. That way would lie certain disaster. If he was lucky he might ward it off once, twice, maybe half a dozen times. But sooner or later, Cloud would get it in place and drag him. There was only one way to prevent that.

Not a word had been spoken after Cloud's grim warning of his intentions. There were no witnesses, and this was Cloud's country. Now, as the loop whipped viciously at him, Stumpy half-fended it from his head, grabbing desperately. Elation surged in him as his fingers closed on the rough fibre of the lariat. Then, moving as fast as Cloud had done a moment before, he was holding to the rope with both hands, walking up it, hand over hand.

Cloud hadn't expected this. He had been prepared for a plea for mercy, for a cringing, beaten man, for almost anything but what was happening. But he was an old-timer when it came to any sort of a scrap. Instantly he touched his ready cayuse with the spurs. Once it had whirled to run, Stumpy would have to let go of the rope in a hurry or be jerked and dragged—not fatally, as in the other case, but enough to knock the wind out of him and leave him a hopeless prey for the next attempt.

Stumpy had foreseen what would be tried, and he was a shade too quick for Cloud, outthinking him as he moved. He reached the horse in time to transfer one hand in a swift lunge and catch a bridle rein, close up to the bit, and the plunging attempt of the cayuse to turn, as the spurs drove bloodily into its sides, only sent it rearing helplessly, with Stumpy maintaining his hold.

Swearing, startled, Cloud grabbed at a quirt and lashed out with it, aiming for Stumpy's face. The next moment, coming up under it, while Cloud's attention was all occupied, Stumpy had reached out and jerked the gun from Cloud's holster.

Pain seared across his scalp, down the side of his neck and raced across his shoulder. The quirt, he knew instantly, was shot-loaded, and it had been wielded with all the vengeful power of Cloud's arm. Stumpy's flattened hat and head of hair had partially protected him, but on his exposed neck the quirt had cut straight through the skin, raising a livid welt, breaking the blood through.

As Stumpy staggered back, Cloud lashed again—a blow aimed for the face. Stumpy's upflung arm took it, saving his eyes, but even at that he was half-blinded for the moment.

He raised the gun, and suddenly seeing what had happened, finding himself without a gun, Cloud dug spurs to his horse again and raced away.

Half-sick with pain, shaken with rage, Stumpy held the gun a minute, then lowered it again. He couldn't shoot a man in the back, and after all, he was winner of this clash.

Winner. But he had felt and tasted some of the blood which turned the moon crimson. And the taste of his own blood was bitter.

CHAPTER 7

THE WORK on the house, barn and homestead shacks had gone forward with a rush. As Chinook put it, that wasn't no sort of a job for a cow waddy to do, so the best thing was to hustle it up and be done with it as soon as possible.

Most of the claim shacks were in place now, snaked along over the smooth cured grass by four or five cayuses, set in place and ready for occupancy. Their furnishings were simple. A sheet-iron stove, which was a combination of cookstove and heater, and which could burn wood or cow chips. A pair of bunks, with blankets, and a bench.

Since these shacks would be used chiefly for sleeping in, not much more was needed, except a few tin dishes, cooking utensils, and a stock of staples, consisting in the main of beans, bacon, flour and salt. With coffee and sugar, and a few cans of tomatoes and peaches for dessert.

This matter of settling down on the land, living on it and finally proving up, was the main issue, and Stumpy knew it. But for the moment it seemed more like a side-show. For things were happening south of the river which drew the attention of the whole country. The nesters, from being scattered, scared individuals, had become a united force. They had a leader at last.

The name of Tom Bannack was on every tongue. Stumpy remembered him as the man he had encountered on the day he left the Wagon Wheel—Bannack, from Dakota, who had promised that if it was trouble that Wolf Masterson was looking for, he would give him plenty of it.

In the comparatively brief time since his arrival, he had organized the frightened nesters, many of whom had been nervous to the point where they were about ready to quit and pull stakes, in obedience to Masterson's warning. Bannack had imbued them with a new confidence and a will to fight.

He had done more than that. He had filed on a quarter-section for himself, had helped the two families who had gone in with him to do the same, and had induced others, hesitant at Fortymile and the fringes of promised land, to come along. Until, all at once, every acre of the spreading range of the Wagon Wheel had been staked and legally filed on, according to the rules made by the federal government.

All of that had been bad enough. But Bannack had added insult to injury by choosing for himself the land whereon the Wagon Wheel buildings stood. Bannack had proclaimed openly that, by the time winter came, he would be occupying those buildings.

To all of that he had added a crowning insult. If the Mastersons wanted to stay on their land, he was willing to marry Gloria and let Wolf stay too. Stumpy's brows twitched together when he heard that.

"He's a fighter, all right," Chinook reported, bringing the news back from Fortymile, along with a wagonload of supplies. "Seems like nobody likes him—he's too bossy and right-down mean for that. But the nesters have been lookin' for a leader, and with Masterson threatenin' to run 'em off, they'll fight behind anybody that can stand up to Wolf."

"Funny there hasn't been a clash already," Stumpy muttered. He was worried by all this news. The fact that he had expected it, knowing it was coming, didn't lessen the impact now. Gloria was there, right in the thick of it, and with Bannack daring even to suggest that she marry him—

"She cut him across the face with her quirt when he told her he'd be willin' to have her for his squaw," Chinook chuckled. "Made him pretty mad, I guess, and he told her he'd have her for that, 'fore he got through with it."

"I'd think Wolf would gun him down, for that," someone ventured.

"Guess he's aimed to, but Bannack's smart," Chinook nodded. "He's kept himself and his men out of sight most of the time, till he could get things set. Wolf and the boys have done a lot of ridin,' lookin' for trouble, but yuh can't shoot a shadow. I guess, from what they done last night, though, there'll be trouble 'most any time."

"What'd they do?"

"Burned a couple of the nesters out. Family men, at that. They couldn't find any of the men-folks at home, no more'n usual lately since Bannack took to managin' things, so they made the women and kids dress, loaded their wagons full of stuff, then fired the buildings and left 'em there."

It was easy to see that Bannack was playing a clever game. He was deliberately going out of his way to inflame Wolf Masterson and the cattlemen, but lying low for the moment, compelling Masterson to do things which would only inflame the nesters against him, getting Wolf in bad while ostensibly remaining law-abiding on his own part.

Bannack's strategy became more apparent a little later, when fresh news drifted up from the south. With the burning of the homestead shacks, the ejection of the women and children, and all the rest of it for evidence, Bannack, accompanied by every man who had filed on a piece of the Wagon Wheel, had gone to court in Fortymile. The federal commissioner, who had been sent there to care for the rush of land-seekers, had taken the only action possible under the circumstances.

He had issued an order to Wolf Masterson to get off the land duly filed on by the homesteaders—to get off it at once, with any of his cattle or other property now unlawfully occupying the premises. Which, in toto, amounted to an order to get off the Wagon Wheel, lock, stock, and barrel.

That was striking below the belt. In common with most of the cattlemen, Wolf Masterson had never been one to ask anybody else to help settle his quarrels—certainly not the courts. His method had always been direct, and he was too old to change.

Now he had promptly replied to the order by declaring that the Wagon Wheel was his, and had sworn to kill any who dared set foot on it henceforth, be they nesters or misguided lawmen who might attempt to enforce that court order.

"And from what I heard, they'll be ridin' out there for a showdown with him tonight," the messenger reported.

Stumpy lost no time. It was already past noon, and it was a long way to the Wagon Wheel. But this was showdown. With the law as well as the nesters behind him, Bannack would lie low no longer. And knowing Wolf Masterson as he did, Stumpy was equally confident that he would do exactly as he had threatened. Tonight the bloody moon would really spill over.

It was the sort of situation which Stumpy had foreseen, the hopelessness of which had caused him to get out from under while the getting was good. But he had to go back there now, no matter how bad the situation. Gloria was there, and from all he had heard, he knew that she would have need of him before this was settled.

He threw a saddle on a horse and started. Just what he would do when he got there was something which would have to be determined at the time. He was classed as a homesteader himself, but he was no friend of the nesters. However, they had the law on their side, and it was no part of his plan to buck the very law which he counted on to win for him, in the game he was playing. Not if he could help it.

But, whatever happened, Gloria came first, above all other plans.

Stumpy lifted his head, staring. He had been riding, lost in thought, paying little attention otherwise. His horse had splashed across the nearly dry Dry Fork, heading on down toward the regular ford of Saddle River, a little way above where the Dry Fork joined it.

Off to the northwest a heavy bank of black clouds tumbled and tossed, looking like a summer thunder-shower, and not long before, a heavy rumble as of thunder had reached his ears. Which was queer, now that he stopped to think of it. Thunder-showers at this season were rare.

But it wasn't that which had caught his attention here. Saddle River itself rolled in front of him, but it was a changed river from the placid, low-water stream which he had crossed before, sadly out of season for this time of year. Ordinarily it was easy to ford it with horses and wagons, the deepest water, near midstream, rolling just around the hubs of the wagon wheels, and the horses splashing through without having to swim.

Evidently it had been that way not more than a few minutes before. For there were seven or eight canvas-topped wagons spread out in a straggling line across the river, one nearly two-thirds of the way across, the others running back to the far bank. And there on the southern bank itself were

two or three others which had not yet started. Nesters'
wagons.

That first glance identified them and their purpose. Ten
wagons in all, starting to cross to the North of Saddle River;
nesters who had come too late to get land on the B in a Box
or even the Wagon Wheel. Like voracious wolves, those
ahead of them had picked that territory clean to the last
bone. So these latecomers, mere vanguards, as they were, of
the ever-increasing horde beginning this new migration,
were encouraged by what Stumpy had done to try the same
thing—to cross Saddle River and take what they could from
Mart Cloud.

Up to this point they had advanced undisturbed. But in
the last minutes—almost the last seconds, apparently, Saddle River itself had changed.

A dirty, ugly crest of water was sweeping down around
the bend, a quarter of a mile upstream, coming like a devour-
ing monster. It spread from shore to shore, a ragged, dirty-
white line broken with scattered bits of drift and seething
in its turbulence, and the shore-line was abruptly sent scamp-
ering on either side, driven back at least a hundred yards
in each direction. That crest of flood water seemed to tower
a yard above the main level of the river.

Thunder—off to the northwest. Rare as it was, there must
have been a downpour off there, a veritable cloudburst,
which had run off, spilled into the river, and was just now
reaching here. Checking his horse, Stumpy watched the
sweep of it, fascinated.

The speed of that crest was much greater than the rest
of the river. Already the stream below it was feeling the
effect, apparent in the sudden, disturbed hurrying of the
water. The crest was spreading out, overlapping itself as it
came, merging with the rest of the river, stirring it to its
same excited turbulence. It was changing from a placid
stream to a raging flood of destruction.

Only a few seconds had ticked away, but in those seconds
the driver of the foremost wagon had seen what was coming.
Now he was trying, frantically, to turn his team and head
back for the southern shore—sure sign that he had lost his
head in the sudden terror of the thing, for that shore was
farther away now than the northern bank.

It was a foolhardy act, induced by panic, and it served to

transmit that same panic to the wagons behind, throwing them into confusion. Stumpy surveyed them grimly. Their one chance would have been to keep going straight ahead. Trying to turn, as they were now, the flood tide was sure to catch them half-turned around, and what would happen then, what was already starting to happen, wasn't pleasant. Though, if that was all the sense they had, maybe they deserved what they'd get.

Then he stared, cursing under his breath. Across the troubled waters came the high, nervous wail of a child, and as the water hit it, Stumpy saw that there were at least two children and a woman in the foremost wagon, besides the driver. They had been hidden inside until the feeling of peril had communicated itself to them, then they had popped into the open like startled gophers.

As they did so, the wagon reeled under the crashing blow of the wall of water, teetered crazily a moment, and went ponderously over on its side. Stumpy dug in the spurs and forced his horse into the river.

CHAPTER 8

THE NEXT few minutes were a nightmare. It was amazing how swiftly and completely the river could change from a sleepy pet to a ravening monster.

Stumpy's own horse could barely swim in the grip of it, and had he not been somewhat upstream from the wagons to start with, able to work outward along with the current, it would have been out of the question to reach any of the hapless victims.

The woman and children had been lucky enough to spill out of the overturned wagon without being caught by it or trapped in that welter of loose, soaked and flappy canvas. But they were like chips upon the river. At least two of the wagons behind them were in equally bad shape, and the horses, tangled in the harness, dragged by the wagons, were struggling frantically, adding to the peril of an already desperate situation.

Stumpy checked his own horse, barely missing being hit by the broken, jagged trunk of a pine tree as it swept past them, then he urged the cayuse forward again. He had glimpsed the straw-colored hair of one of the children, a girl of about ten or twelve, and he managed to reach out and grab her by the hair, then to pull her to the saddle in front of him.

She looked to be half-drowned, but she was still conscious, and as her wide, terrified blue eyes met his for a moment, hope came back to them. Docilely enough she submitted, without struggling, and Stumpy marveled a little at her courage in such a moment.

But he was doubly thankful, for, off thirty feet or so, he saw the woman and the other child, the mother swimming feebly and trying desperately to hold her child to her and keep her head above water at the same time. It was a losing battle which she fought, and Stumpy saw instantly that, with more cluttered debris sweeping down at them, they could neither miss it nor keep afloat till he could reach them.

Already he had shaken out his lariat, as Mart Cloud had done a few days before, but with a different purpose. Now he sent it sweeping out, saw the loop settle around the shoulders of the woman, and instantly urged his horse to more desperate efforts, taking a quick half-hitch of the end of the rope around the saddle-horn.

To escape that pile of floating death, made up of broken wood, they must head straight upstream, into the full teeth of the flood. Stumpy slid off into the water, below his struggling cayuse, holding to the rope and horn with one hand, and with the other helping to steady the girl already there. He caught a mouthful of water which nearly strangled him, as a wave-crest swept over his head.

He came up, swimming desperately, saw the debris pass, and pulled hard on the rope, bringing them across to the saddle. A few moments later, moments that had stretched like hours, they reached shallow water, which had been dry bank ten minutes before, scrambled and splashed another hundred yards to firm ground beyond.

Once on hard ground, the horse stood panting with drooping head, all but exhausted by the terrible but gallant struggle it had put up there. Stumpy lifted down the half-drowned children and their mother. Like his horse, he saw that they were near exhaustion, but alive. And out there in the river, hell still held control over a quarter-mile deep area, where men and horses and even other women and children struggled in wild confusion.

Of those who were finally rescued and gotten back to the shore, nearly all were in pitiful shape. Soaked, half-drowned, on the verge of exhaustion, chilled and shivering in the wind, with no dry clothes or anything else left for many of them, they were like lost children who did not know what to do or where to turn.

These folks had to have fire and shelter, and have it soon —otherwise many of them, the women and children especially, would have found a speedier and kindlier but no more certain end if left in the river.

An axe was tied to the back of one of the wagons now on the shore. Stumpy jerked it loose, ran to a pile of driftwood on the bank, piled there by an even higher flood tide than this one had been, and so above the water. Knocking in to it, he found dry wood, and yelled to one of the men to bring matches and get a fire going.

Under the driving force of him, the huddled refugees stirred to action. Soon there was a roaring fire, and the women and children were gathered in the grateful heat of it.

It was getting dark. The woman whom Stumpy had rescued at the first, came now to protest.

"I don't know your name," she said. "But you've worked like ten men, to help us—and I guess we owe about everything to you, including our lives. But you've still got your own wet clothes on. You need to rest up and get warm, the next thing."

"I'm fine," Stumpy started to protest, but she silenced him by bringing dry clothes which had been rustled up from one of the wagons and waving him to the wagon to change. Shaking with the cold as soon as he paused for a moment, Stumpy obeyed, then gulped down more of the scalding coffee.

The excitement and effort had kept them going for a while. Now followed a let-down, for taking stock was a dismal business. Five wagons and all their equipment lost, one man gone. Another man with a broken arm, a child who shivered continually with a chill.

At least five people owed their lives directly to Stumpy, and there was satisfaction in the thought that he had been able to help. But if there had been trouble at the Wagon Wheel it would be over with now, one way or another, and he had been unable to get there, to help Gloria when she would be most in need of his aid. And that sudden flash flood which had struck—that was funny. Mighty funny.

He got away from them, answering as few questions as possible, his mind troubled by questions about the Wagon Wheel and what might have befallen there. No need to go on there now. In any case, that battle in the river and the subsequent exertions he had put forth had left him nearly exhausted. He'd get back to the Saddle, get some sleep, and then see how things were shaping up.

He recrossed the river, and almost bumped into another shadowy horseman. This man chuckled hoarsely.

"That sure stopped the damn nesters, didn't it?" he asked. "Teach 'em better than to monkey with Mart Cloud, I reckon. Blowin' up that dam spoils his irrigatin' notions for another year, but it'll show 'em that there's only death waitin' North of Saddle River."

The other man, who was plainly one of Cloud's riders, had spoken in the easy conviction that any horseman moving hereabouts at that hour was another of the same crew. He had vanished in the gloom now, and Stumpy did not disillusion him. But he had gone hot and cold at the news.

That thunder, then, had been man-made, dynamite tearing out an earth-fill. This was the first that Stumpy had known, that Cloud had built such a dam, with plans for irrigating dry land later on. But today he had been willing to sacrifice that project if in so doing he could stop the homeseekers. The murder of women and children was apparently incidental, insofar as the boss of the Longhorn was concerned.

It had been well timed, that blast, set when this caravan of nesters had been discovered heading toward Saddle River, then touched off on signal from some watcher. Timed for murder.

"The fool," Stumpy muttered. "I at least figured he had common sense. But when this gets known—"

He shook his head, leaving the thought unfinished. The wrath of the weak could be a terrible thing when it was provoked by such wanton onslaughts, and there was Tom Bannack to lead the homesteaders. Bannack was the sort of man who loved a good fight, who craved power even as these early cattle kings had craved it. So long as there was trouble in the country, he wasn't one to be content merely to plow his own acres.

It was a miserable night, the darkness almost absolute, so Stumpy gave his horse its head, knowing that it would find its way home when he could not.

Snow carpeted the country the next morning, a couple of inches of white which would soon melt, but it gave a wintry touch to the landscape. The trees and bushes were laden with it, clothed in beauty.

A little past noon, with the sun bright overhead and snow lingering only on the higher peaks, fresh news arrived from south of the river. Disquieting news.

Wolf Masterson had put up a battle, as he had threatened to do. But the law, with the homesteaders for a posse, had moved in on him, and his crew had been outnumbered more than two to one. Likewise, it appeared that Tom Bannack had proven his right to leadership by a good display of generalship. They had outflanked the Wagon Wheel crew, surprised them, and made Masterson a prisoner almost before the fight was well under way.

That had pretty well nipped the fight in the bud, and now Wolf Masterson was in jail at Fortymile, facing an array of serious charges. These included armed resistance to officers of the law, defying the edict of the federal government, and various other things.

Along with that, the Wagon Wheel had been effectively taken over by the nesters, and as a ranch and a cattle outfit it had automatically ceased to exist.

Of Gloria there was no news. Again, losing no time, Stumpy started out. The thing that he had foreseen and had been preparing for had come. The only difference was that it had happened sooner than he had expected. But he was ready, and now was the time to act.

At the river, he saw that the homeseekers were still camped where he had left them the night before, on the southern bank. They had apparently made no further move to cross it, nor, from all appearances, had they been molested by Cloud's Longhorn crew. But there was one significant change. Several more wagonloads of like-minded landless families had joined them.

This was the only good crossing anywhere close by, so, being in no mood for delays, Stumpy crossed. By the time he was halfway over, however, he had been recognized, and nearly every man in the camp was coming out and waiting for him as he made the shore.

"You still aiming to try and take some of the land, off across there?" Stumpy asked, nodding toward the northern bank.

"Sure. Why not?" That was Eric Johnson, one of the newcomers to the camp. "You proved that it could be done, Mr. Garford. And after the dirty, stinkin' trick that Cloud pulled on these folks here yesterday—well, we ain't stoppin' till we've run him out of this country, just the same as Wolf Masterson had been run off south of the river. Damn all cattlemen anyway, say I."

So they had learned of the murderous trick which Cloud played on them. It was only natural that it should come to light, and the effect was precisely as Stumpy had foreseen. Instead of frightening them away, it had served to rouse their anger and determination to a fighting pitch.

"I don't blame you any," he confessed. "It was a dirty trick. But don't make any mistake about it—you're going up against a tough proposition in Mart Cloud. He aims to fight. And he don't care what method he uses."

"He's shown that, plain enough," Johnson agreed. "But here's what we sort of had in mind, Mr. Garford—"

"Cut out the Mister," Stumpy suggested.

"Sure. Here's what we had in mind, Stumpy. You went up there and took land, and showed that it could be done. Cloud has sworn to run you off—so yuh're in the same boat, along with the rest of us. We need help, there ain't no denyin' that, but you can stand some more too, till Cloud is run plumb out of the country, or killed. When we get it so there ain't a cattleman nor a critter in this whole country—"

Stumpy's mind had been far away, picturing what had happened, and other things that might have happened, down on the Wagon Wheel. Wolf Masterson had had it coming to him, maybe, but the fact remained that it was the cattlemen who had pioneered this country, doing the necessary work to make it safe for other white men to live in. Masterson had made a home there, working hard through the years, confident that the range would remain as open in years to come as it had in years past.

That was where he had made his mistake. But you couldn't blame a man for fighting for what he had spent a lifetime in building. And like him, Stumpy was a cattleman. Johnson's last words jerked him abruptly back.

"Don't forget, I'm a cattleman myself," Stumpy said harshly. He'd helped these people when their need was a dire one, and he could sympathize with them now. But they were of the same sort who had run Masterson off the Wagon Wheel, who had done no telling what to Gloria. And his sympathies were surging strongly toward those with whom his lot had always been cast.

"I'm a cattleman," he repeated. "And get this, Johnson. I aim to keep on being one. We aren't allies, and it's noways likely that we ever could be." While they stared at him, startled and shocked, he dug in the spurs and was gone.

CHAPTER 9

FORTYMILE HAD changed in the comparatively short time since Stumpy had seen it last, the day when he had pulled out of there with his cowboy crew of homesteaders and caravan of wagons. Since then he had stuck to the Saddle, sending others to town for the necessary supplies. And though the transition of Fortymile had been under way before, the completeness of it somehow shocked him now.

It had been founded as a cow town, and a cow town it had been for more than a quarter of a century. Now, in a brief span of weeks, it had ceased to be a cow town, had become something quite different and somehow alien.

There were still the same buildings on the same streets, the chewed hitchrails, the big watering trough under a grove of tall cottonwoods, and all the rest of it. Outwardly and physically there was little change, save that most of the cow ponies which had formerly lined the hitchrails were absent, their places taken by teams of heavy work horses attached to buggies and spring wagons, or the big wagons of the homesteaders, denuded now for the most part of their canvas tops. Though these were small changes in themselves.

It was the population, the spirit of the town, which had altered so radically. The cattlemen from south of the river were gone, and the business men had been quick to recognize that fact. So, too, had the court house crowd.

Secretly they might dab the edges of frayed sleeves at

suspicious moisture and sigh for the days that were gone, but openly they had changed with the times. If they wanted to make a living and stay on in this country, there was nothing else for them to do. Homesteaders, small farmers, made up the crowds who now thronged the streets and filled the stores. This was Saturday evening, and the town was full.

Full in a new sense. There was far less patronage for the saloons than would have been the case with an equal crowd of cowboys, and that, Stumpy conceded, was a change for the better. A cowboy seldom got to town often, and when he did, he liked to celebrate. These men, for the most part, were family men, with a sense of responsibility, and desperately poor, as they sought to make a start toward a home in a raw land. Besides, they could get to town far more often than a cowboy.

But there was a sense of celebration in town tonight; a quiet but still jubilant hilarity, to mark the victory that had been so complete, south of the river. It was that, and the fact that it could go so unchallenged, which marked the transition of Fortymile from one sort of town to another. Its frontier period, its wild days, were ended. Henceforth it would be a staid, respectable village.

It was late afternoon when Stumpy reached it. He ate supper at a restaurant, conscious that he was being pointed out by people whom he didn't know, to other people who were new to him, and being discussed. As the man who had defied the tradition and gone north of Saddle River, he was something of a personage, even among the homesteaders. The news, too, of what he had done the day before, to help the nesters at the river, had reached town, and for the most part he was looked upon with a kindly eye.

Which wasn't exactly pleasing. It placed him in a position of being neither fish nor fowl, and Stumpy resented that. Inquiries revealed that Wolf Masterson was still in jail, and likely to remain there. The big cattle herd of the Wagon Wheel had been rounded up, and was still somewhere out on its former range, with Gloria and a good part of the old crew to look after it.

That much was known. The speculation concerning that same herd filled Stumpy with increasing uneasiness. There were a couple thousand head of cattle, and they were on their way—but without the slightest idea of where they could go.

"The homesteaders have the Wagon Wheel, now," Curt Tucker, proprietor of the hardware store and an old friend of Stumpy's, explained. "And they've told the crew tuh get the herd off their land, by dawn tomorrow—to get 'em off and keep 'em off, every hoof. But how in blazes can they do it, when there ain't nowhere to go, except on to other homestead land, which counts the same?"

"Dawn tomorrow, eh?" Stumpy nodded. "That ain't leavin' them much time to make a change—seein' that the law threw Masterson off only last night."

Tucker looked quickly, rather furtively around the big, now deserted store, and lowered his voice a little.

"It's a blasted mean trick," he said hoarsely. "Way it looks tuh me, these nesters—meanin' Tom Bannack—are out not only to run Masterson off his land, but tuh put him plumb out of business, too—robbin' him blind."

"How?"

"It's simple, the way they're workin' it. First they take over the ranch and get him arrested. Then I guess they went ahead and helped themselves to everything on the home place. From what I hear, Bannack made good his boast, and moved in to Wolf's house, takin' everything in it for himself."

"And he's getting away with it?"

"Seems so. Now he sets this deadline, figgerin' that there's only a girl to look after the stock, and there ain't nary chance of her meetin' the deadline, since there's nowhere to go with the cattle. I hear there's a hombre named Trebold got in here this afternoon, and that he's a cattle buyer. Workin' hand in glove with Bannack, from what I can find out. He'll show up in the mornin' and offer tuh buy the cattle for about a quarter of what they're worth. And my idea is that him and Bannack aim tuh split the profits—'less she takes Bannack's other offer."

"What's that?" Stumpy asked sharply.

"If she'll marry Bannack, so he gets the herd anyway, why, he figures to win either way."

So that was it. As Stumpy had suspected from the first, Bannack was not only a leader and a fighter, but a man utterly without scruple; one who had seen a chance for profit on a huge scale, and had cut himself in by the simple expedient of coming to take up a homestead and make himself leader of men sadly in need of a leader. And in the doing of it, he aimed to set up for himself a greater empire than the cattlemen had enjoyed.

"It's a nice scheme—if he can get away with it," Stumpy commented drily.

"What's there to stop him?" demanded Tucker a little hopelessly. "Since he's led the men tuh victory over Masterson, most all of them are eatin' out of his hand. If there was a vote in this country tomorrow, he could get four out of every five, for anything he wanted. With that sort of a situation, he can do just about anything he pleases. And all that he's lacked, up to now, is money. By tomorrow, with the cattle, he figures to have plenty of that, too."

"He hasn't got that herd—yet," Stumpy said softly. "And that reminds me, I've got some work to do. Be seeing you, Curt."

Tucker remained staring after him as he left the store and swung onto his horse again. Just what did Stumpy have in mind, anyway? Tom Bannack was a man to be reckoned with in this country, of that there was no longer any question. But Stumpy Garford, the man who could go North of Saddle River and make it stick—he too was a man to reckon with.

"And them two'll be clashin' head on, one of these days, or I'm more of a dodderin' old fool than I ever suspected before," Tucker nodded to himself. "When they do—well, it'll be right int'restin' tuh watch, I reckon."

Tonight, by contrast with the previous evening, it was clear and cold. The snow had all melted during the day, the wind had whispered away in the west, and utter stillness held the night as Stumpy rode out of town. Pale, cold stars looked down, and Stumpy estimated that there would be ice fringing the creeks and creeping across the ponds before the dawn. There might be a scant respite still of Indian summer, but winter was definitely on the march.

He had hardly left the town when a pound of hoofs sounded and another horseman pulled alongside. Even in the gloom, it was easy for Stumpy to see that the man was a tenderfoot. He jounced in the saddle, arms working back and forth like pistons, and sawed his horse to a walk with an audible sigh of relief.

"Friend," he said. "Could you direct me to what has been known as the Wagon Wheel ranch? I find myself a little confused in this country, especially after dark, but I need to get out there without delay."

His voice was high and reedy, and spoken mostly through the nose. Stumpy sighed resignedly. He would have preferred to ride alone, but he supposed he could stand company if he had to.

"I'm going that way, myself," he explained.

"That is most fortunate, to have a guide who knows this country. I suppose that, soon now, as these homesteads are developed, there will be well-marked roads running everywhere. It will be a great blessing."

"Likely there'll be plenty roads," Stumpy conceded. As to how much of a blessing it would be, he reserved judgment.

"And the big herds of cattle will be gone," the stranger continued. "Gone before the march of progress. I suppose I should be sorry, since for the moment at least I am a cattle buyer."

So this was Trebold. Already he had given himself away. He was no more a cattle buyer than he was a cattleman. At the most, he was acting as an agent for Bannack.

Stumpy turned in the saddle. His voice was cold, deliberate.

"Reckon I made a little mistake," he said. "This ain't the way to the Wagon Wheel."

Trebold pulled his horse to a stop and stared.

"Eh? A mistake—"

"Or to put it plainer, the Wagon Wheel does lie out this way—but it ain't the way for you to be ridin'. You won't be doing any business out there tonight, or in the morning, either."

Trebold blinked nervously.

"I'm afraid I don't understand—"

"I'm tryin' to save you a ride that I can see you ain't enjoyin' any," Stumpy said drily. "You're headin' out there, figgerin' to buy the herd of the Wagon Wheel, come morning. It's wasted effort. They aren't going to be sold."

"Not going to be sold? But I was given to understand— Mr. Bannack told me—I mean—"

"I know what you mean. But Bannack was mistaken. They

aren't going to be sold. So you're wastin' your time, ridin' this way at all. In fact, considerin' the mood that the Wagon Wheel punchers are going to be in, I wouldn't want to risk gettin' close to them with any such fool suggestion. I don't say that they'd tar and feather you, since tar and feathers ain't always easy to come at. And they might not string you up to the nearest cottonwood. But if I was you, I wouldn't risk displeasin' them needless."

Trebold looked wildly around.

"You—you're sure—"

"The only thing I'm sure of is, that I'd hate to be in your boots if you made a picayunish offer like you was aimin' to, the mood they'll be in. It'd be plumb temptin' fate."

"In that case, I—I think I'll take your advice and go back to town," Trebold decided. He started to saw his horse around, halted again. "You are certain—how can you be sure of this?"

"Plumb certain," Stumpy nodded. "And I'm sure that those cattle won't be for sale, because I'm takin' charge of them myself. If you're still curious, I'll tell you my name. Maybe it won't answer your question, and then again, it may shine light on a few gloomy places. I'm Stumpy Garford."

Trebold was staring at him, mouth half open, much as though he had seen a ghost. Suddenly he turned his horse and was jouncing wildly back toward the lights of Forty-mile.

Grinning a little for the first time that day, Stumpy rode on. He could at least enjoy the peace of the night now, and it was like balm to his soul. This was still open range, but it would soon be enclosed with fences on every hand, and the moving Wagon Wheel was probably the last big herd which would ever traverse this land.

But there would be homes and schools, and other things. Stumpy shook his head. It wasn't up to him to say which mode of life was best. Only he had his own preferences, and, knowing the country, he felt about as sorry for the average tenderfoot who sought to wrest a living from a hundred and sixty acres in here, as he did for the cattle kings who had lost their crowns.

It was close to midnight when he came again to the disintegrating Wagon Wheel. Then, ahead, he saw a familiar dark blot which he knew was the big herd, mostly bedded down now for the night. In the distance was a chuck wagon, and hobbled horses not far off. With the dawn, they had to move—and he could sense the heavy hopelessness, the sense of foreboding which must disturb the uneasy slumbers of these men tonight. For where could they move?

He approached the herd, saw the shadowy silhouette of a horse and rider on night herd, was challenged sharply as he approached.

"Stop right there! Who are you and what do you want?"

Sudden relief surged through Stumpy. Gloria, helping to keep a sharp eye on her own herd. At least, nothing had happened to her.

"It's me, Gloria," he said softly. "Stumpy."

He heard the sudden catch in her breath, saw her half-turn, eagerly, at the sound of his voice. Then, as quickly, she had stiffened in the saddle, her voice came icy and remote.

"You'd better ride somewhere else, Mr. Stumpy Garford. This is a cattleman's spread, and you wouldn't feel at home here. Go on over where you'll be welcome—among your fellow-squatters."

CHAPTER 10

THE SCORN and contempt in her voice were not quite enough to hide the hurt down underneath. The words stung, but Stumpy wasn't thinking as much about them as about this girl, feeling herself friendless and alone in a suddenly bleak world, gamely trying to carry on.

"Feel better, now you've got that off your chest, Gloria?" he asked, and she had a feeling that he must be grinning at her. There was something warm and reassuring in the tones of his voice, more than in the words themselves.

"I know just how you feel, after all that's been happenin', Gloria, and I sure can't blame you a mite," Stumpy went on. "But don't get me wrong. I told you that when you needed a friend, I'd be around, and I figure this is the time."

"I don't need a friend of your caliber," she flashed at him. "The Wagon Wheel has no use for nesters."

Brave words, but there was a catch in her voice, a not quite convincing something which Stumpy was quick to note. He rode a little closer.

"You've been pretty good friends with the Hankins and

some of the others," he reminded her. "Not because you had any liking for them settling on the Wagon Wheel, but because they were human beings who were trying hard to make a living, the only way they knew how, and you felt sorry for them. Maybe you've heard how I tried to help some others out last night. But it was for the same sort of a reason, Gloria. Not because I had any use for them or what they represented."

"But you're doing the same thing—homesteading around like any of these other nesters." Gloria's voice was a little doubtful.

"Nope, not like these others," Stumpy protested soberly. "I'm like your dad, Gloria, like you are—a cattleman. That's what I've always been figurin' on for a job, the only thing I know or would be worth a tinker's darn at. I—"

"It's not a darn, it's a tinker's dam," Gloria interrupted. "And it's not a swear word, it's kind of a little instrument or something that they used to use."

Stumpy grinned to himself. He had known what her reaction to the word would be when he used it. Gloria was getting to be herself again.

"Sure. Well, I wouldn't be worth a tinker's dam at anything else. But, like I told your father, I could see what was going to happen in this country, with the nesters flockin' in. I'd of liked to help him save the Wagon Wheel, but you know how Wolf is—proud-like, and he wouldn't listen to me—"

"I know," Gloria agreed, low-voiced. "And now they—they've got him in jail!"

"Where they won't keep him long," Stumpy said comfortably. "But that was the situation. I was sure, when the nesters got to comin' in here so thick, and when they run Old Man Proctor right off the B, that something pretty much like it would be happenin' to the Wagon Wheel, before it had made many more turns. Only thing that fooled me was, it took place a lot faster than I thought it would."

"I guess it fooled us all, there," Gloria confessed. "Though you were the only one to see what was coming."

"Well, I've been down in homestead country, a few years back, and maybe that give me a better idea than some of the old-timers in here had," Stumpy suggested. "But that was why I got out, and it was why I used the nesters' own weapon—since it's the only one you can fight 'em with. I went

North of Saddle River for two reasons. One, it was the only country where I could get a big chunk of land, all together, and besides, I knew that if I didn't, the others would, pretty soon. I even tried to show Mart Cloud how he could save part of his spread, before it was too late. But he was too stubborn to take my advice—up to now, at least."

"I've heard how you licked him," Gloria said. "I—I was proud of you, Stumpy."

"It was a right dangerous proceedin', going up there," Stumpy nodded. "But there wasn't any choice. It was the only good land right handy, and I had to have some, without no fooling—have it ready for this."

"What do you mean?"

"For what's happened here." He waved an inclusive hand at the herd. "You know what Bannack aims to do next?"

"I don't know." Her voice held a discouraged ring to it. "But I'm sure that it will be something nasty. He has got all the homesteaders together, and told us that we have to get off by morning, with every head of cattle. And where can we go, with every place taken? But what does he plan?"

"He aimed to buy your stock, through a fake buyer, for about a quarter of what they are worth. Figurin' that when you couldn't move them and had to do it, you'd have to sell."

Gloria's chin came up.

"He can think again!" she said fiercely. "I don't know what we'll do—but Bannack will never get them."

"I guess he had another offer to make—about lettin' you and the cattle stay on the Wagon Wheel, if you'd marry him."

Gloria colored angrily, then her cheeks grew white.

"He insulted me once before with such an offer!" she said. "I'd sooner lose everything than that!"

"Naturally," Stumpy agreed. "What we'll do, Gloria, is get the herd to moving. Up to my Saddle Ranch. There's plenty grass there, and no cattle to eat it. That's what I got it for, Gloria."

She stared at him, excited and startled, as though seeing him for the first time.

"Stumpy! Oh—I don't know what to say to you—"

She was crying, suddenly distraught in her relief. Stumpy rode a little closer, so that her head was against the roughness of his coat, and he patted her shoulder gently.

"It's all right, Gloria. Me, I wanted a ranch, and I saw a chance to get it. And I knew it'd take a long time to get a herd, but here was going to be a herd that'd need a ranch—so it looked like the sensible thing to be ready. We can be partners, sort of—if you like the idea."

"Like it?" Her eyes were shining through tears as she lifted her head again. "Stumpy, you're a life-saver. The Wagon Wheel would be lost—lost completely, without this, now."

"I don't know how your dad will feel about takin' the cattle up to the Saddle," Stumpy said, after a moment of silence. "I reckon he don't just like me these days—"

"I don't see how he can help liking it, in a case like this," Gloria declared. "Anyway, the cattle will there before he has anything to say about it. I own a two-fifths interest in them, and with Dad in—in jail, I'm in charge, of course."

"I reckon you are," Stumpy agreed. He laughed suddenly. "Bannack is going to be right disappointed, come morning. A herd like this is rich pickings to have slip through your fingers."

"He wouldn't have gotten them anyway," Gloria declared. "Though what we could have done is more than I know. The boys all discussed it last evening, and I've been racking my brains for hours, but I couldn't see any way out."

"Most of the boys still here?" Stumpy asked.

"Two of them are in the hospital, but the others are all here—and fighting mad. They want to go to town and storm the jail to get Dad out. I had a hard time to make them agree to wait till morning before doing anything. But I told them that they had to be on hand if things started to happen here. After that—well, I don't know just how I'll manage to control them."

"I'll talk to them," Stumpy said. He felt a warmness around his heart. Such headstrong methods would be disastrous right now, with Wolf Masterson a federal prisoner. But the boys had the right idea to start with. They were loyal to the core, disdainful of the cost. He had been one with them for a long time, and it was nice to think of them now.

"But what can we do, about Dad?" Gloria asked. "He—he's so headstrong, Stumpy. And this fight, and all—they have some terribly serious charges against him, and I—I'm afraid. And he wouldn't ever stand it to be shut up behind the bars, not for long. It would kill him."

"Come hard on him, I guess," Stumpy conceded. "But I'll ride in to town in the morning again and see if I can't do something. Ought to be able to get him out on bail."

"Maybe." Her voice was doubtful. "But it'll be pretty stiff —and I don't know how we'd raise it, Stumpy. With what's happened, we haven't a cent. Of course, we might be able to mortgage the cattle—"

"We won't cross that bridge till we come to it," Stumpy said easily. "And I reckon it would be a good idea to rout the boys out now. Course, they need their beauty sleep, but the sooner we get this herd to movin', the better all around."

Gloria agreed readily, and they rode across to the camp. Tents had been set up, in lieu of the bunkhouses from which the crew had been so unceremoniously ejected, and Stumpy had them awake and out in a matter of minutes. Already a cook fire was burning, a red beacon in a sea of blackness, and they gathered around sleepily, exclaiming a little at sight of Stumpy. Gloria briefly outlined what Stumpy had offered, and what was to be done.

"And we want to get started right away," she ended.

One of the punchers scratched his chin.

"Sounds all right," he agreed. "Only—we got kind of pressin' business in town."

"If you go strayin' off and let a bunch of nesters grab these cattle and get away with them, Wolf will have your hides when he gets out," Stumpy warned them. "You get them headed for Saddle River, without losin' any time. And don't let anybody stop you. One of you ride on ahead and tell Chinook to have my crew meet you at the river, so there'll be no trouble from Mart Cloud. That clear?"

"Plenty," the dissenter agreed laconically. "But where'll you be—and how about the boss?"

"I'll be in town, getting him out of jail," Stumpy said, equally laconic. "Any objections?"

"Dog-gone, I reckon mebby you're the man to do it!" They gave in, and Stumpy waved a cheerful farewell to Gloria and turned off toward Fortymile again. But once out of sight in the graying dawn, his face was bleak and troubled again. Some of these other jobs had been tough enough—but they looked mild in comparison to the one he had so lightly promised to do now.

CHAPTER 11

CLIFF VAUGHAN had been sheriff at Fortymile for a decade, and he made a good officer. During the years he had been elected by the vote of the cattlemen, and he had been raised as a cowboy himself. But like the others at Fortymile, he was aware now of the change, and the fact that the cattlemen's vote was fast becoming like the dodo bird.

He received Stumpy cordially, as he did with every friend, but this cordiality covered no commitments, as Stumpy was well aware.

"I hear you're getting to be a big landholder on your own, Stumpy," the sheriff said. "And North of Saddle River, at that. Just when most of the ranches are getting split up, you come along and show us a new wrinkle in getting a big one."

"Me, I'm apt to have a lot of new wrinkles before I get done with this job," Stumpy grinned, then sobered. "Any chances of getting Wolf Masterson out of jail, Cliff?"

"I've always counted it as a pretty stout jail."

"I saw the Wagon Wheel crew this morning. They were in a mood to take your jail apart, Cliff. But I persuaded them that it wasn't the thing to do."

The sheriff nodded.

"I've been kind of concerned that they'd try something like that," he admitted. "And I'm obliged to you, Stumpy. But as to Masterson, now—those are pretty serious charges against him. He didn't just go out to buck me and the law I represent. I ain't a proud man, and I could maybe overlook a few things, considerin' the pesterin' he's been up against. But when he goes and tangles with a federal ruling—that makes it bad."

"Then you can't do anything for him?"

Vaughan shook his head.

"It's plumb out of my hands, Stumpy. I'd like to. But your only chance, way it looks to me, would be to see the Judge. Maybe Quayle can fix it. Though I wouldn't bank too much on that till I found out."

Judge Quayle had been district judge even before Vaughan's day as sheriff. He was a hale, hearty man in his early sixties, and he listened gravely, nodding.

"Maybe we can fix something up," he said. "I've got

53

enough authority to handle the case, I guess. And I'd like to do it. Wolf and me, we've had our run-ins—show me a man that Wolf hasn't had trouble with, one time or another—but for all that, we've been pretty good friends. But he's got in pretty deep, this time."

"You can't rightly blame him, can you?"

"Not for defendin' his home, no. But he ought to use a little judgment about how he does it. Main thing I'm afraid of, if we do fix bail and let him out, is what he'll do then. Might be safer to keep him shut up for awhile, so he can't kick over the traces and make it any worse."

"I reckon you're right, there, Judge. Just the same, if it can be fixed up, now—"

"That will depend on whether his friends can raise the bail money. I understand that he's lost about everything he had, except his cattle, the last few days. Which is too bad. But some folks can never see what's coming till it hits them. Because they ranged their stock here for twenty or thirty years, a lot of these old-timers actually believed that the land belonged to them. They've had it all these years without paying a cent of taxes, and naturally the government wants to see somebody really own it, so that they will pay taxes."

"What's the bail worth?"

"Have to make it pretty steep, or they'd have my scalp—with charges like he's got against him. Five thousand ought to do it, though."

He glanced keenly at Stumpy, but the cattleman's face betrayed no emotion. Inwardly Stumpy was a little shocked. He had a strong hunch that the Judge had placed the figure so high that he was certain it could not be raised now, under the circumstances. And it was steep. If he raised the money, it would strain his resources to do it, leaving him broke, without money for operations.

Awhile back, he had offered Mart Cloud ten thousand for land, but since that time he had spent a lot of money. Stumpy calculated rapidly. He could send a wire to Baldy, his partner—

But Baldy was a prospector, first, last and always. Right now, by virtue of the strike which he had made awhile back, he had been raised to the more dignified status of miner, employing several men to do the work, and not having much to do except oversee the job and help spend the money that came rolling out.

For a couple of weeks, Baldy had been transported to heights long dreamed of. He had even taken a trip to San Francisco, declaring that he was going to paint the town red, then mebby go on to Paris and really see the world. No longer was he a penniless prospector. Now he was a moneyed man, a gentleman of leisure, one who could see the world.

It had worked out just about as Stumpy had known it would. Baldy had aimed to spend at least a month in San Francisco. He had been back in two weeks, including the time spent in coming and going, and already he had his fill of the bright lights. Nothing more was said about Paris.

After that brief splurge, he had been happy to get back to the mine and the job of overseeing it again. But that would soon pall on him. It was extremely doubtful if he would stay around there long, since the foreman was trustworthy and perfectly capable of looking after things. Baldy was more at home with a burro than with his fellow human-beings. Any day now, he'd be getting a pack together and heading out into the desert again.

No longer would the necessity for getting a stake drive him, but he could prospect much the same as before, and probably would. Once the desert had swallowed him, it might be weeks or months before any one would hear from him again.

If that had happened already—and it might easily have done so—then a wire sent to the mine would be as useless as a will o' the wisp. And Stumpy needed assistance from his partner, needed it in a hurry. However, there didn't seem to be anything else to do, except take the chance.

"I'll try and get the money raked up this afternoon," Stumpy promised. "But how long will it be necessary to keep it tied up, Judge? I'll admit that I could use the money for other things, right about now."

Judge Quayle chuckled comfortably.

"Who couldn't?" he asked. "But I'll arrange bail, then, and hold the hearing in a couple of days. I don't know how things will work out at the hearing, of course, but if he can be convincing enough, and promise not to kick over the traces any more, maybe we can get these charges quashed. In which case, your money would be released again. And if they can't be quashed—well, when he's out, maybe he can raise his own bail for the rest of the time it's needed."

That, of course, was as far as the judge could go, and Stumpy was grateful. He sent off the telegram, thankful for once that Fortymile was sufficiently civilized so that it had a line of poles and wire reaching in from the outer world. For a decade now it had expected the railroad to come, but the line of steel seemed as far distant as ever.

The telegram would go south for fifty miles, swing east for nearly a hundred, follow another line south, and then westward, coming finally to the town nearest where the mine and, with luck, Baldy as well, were located. From the end of the wire to the mine was an added twenty miles, and Stumpy added instructions and money for the message to be taken out to the mine at once. Otherwise it might lie in a cubbyhole of the post office for a week before anyone came in from the mine to pick it up.

That attended to, Stumpy set about the business of scraping together the five thousand in cash. Which was not so easy, and required most of the day before he had it all together.

By now, the Wagon Wheel herd should have reached Saddle River, and they ought to be across it before darkfall. That would put them on his own range, where they would be safe, with the combined crews to look after them.

A lumber wagon was swinging down the street, pulling to a stop in front of Doc Barker's office. Hay had been piled in the bottom of the wagon, and on this lay three men who were now being unloaded. All of them appeared to be badly shot up, and at least two of them were unconscious—or worse. Nesters, from the looks of things.

"What's been going on?" Stumpy asked the driver, as he turned to lend a hand.

"Hell broke loose, up at Saddle River," the driver explained. "We got across, and run into Cloud's gun-crew."

CHAPTER 12

EXCITEMENT surged through Fortymile like a stampeding herd. The abortive clash of the nesters with Wolf Masterson and his Wagon Wheel crew, a couple of days before, had been an easy victory, which had merely whetted their appetites. But today it had been something different.

Tom Bannack was not a man to let grass grow under his feet. With his followers flushed by that easy triumph, he had sought to lead them on to new glories, and the thing that had happened at the river, the flood which Cloud had unloosed on some of their fellow home-seekers, had been the needed spur.

So today Bannack had gone up there to take personal charge, and with him he had taken a considerable crew of nesters, both newcomers who had yet to find land, and others who had helped to overrun the Wagon Wheel but who were ready for more excitement.

Bannack had been in a savage mood. He had counted the Wagon Wheel cattle as good as his own, the day before, had figured that he had them safely trapped, with nowhere to go. Gloria would have to accept one of his two alternatives, and he didn't much care which one, for both led toward the same inevitable end.

Arriving, at the dawn deadline, confident of finishing the business, he had found the big herd gone. When they had finally come up with them, the cattle were steadily on the move, heading north.

It had done no good to challenge them, to declare that they couldn't keep moving over land already homesteaded. The crew of the Wagon Wheel had laughed at them, and invited them to try and stop them. They were spoiling for a fight, and there was nothing to do but let them go on.

Temporarily balked, vengeful, Bannack had promptly turned to this other project, and with a double purpose in mind. If he could get his own crew safely across Saddle River, he would be in a position from there to do something about this same herd of cattle when they came along.

The handful of nesters who had remained camped at the edge of the river, since their disastrous experience with it, were grateful for help, ready to move with others when strong reinforcements arrived. But this time, under Bannack's leadership, they did not make the mistake of starting across with their wagons and all their worldly goods. Instead, leaving wagons and women and children safely in camp, the men, mounted on plow horses or whatever sort of cayuse could be found, armed and determined, had crossed the river and swung west on to the Longhorn spread.

Triumph surged through them as they rode for a mile

without opposition. And then, all at once, they had found themselves in the midst of a withering gun-fire, coming from in front and on both sides. They had ridden straight into ambush.

As the driver of the wagon had so graphically informed Stumpy, hell had broken loose. Mart Cloud had made good his boast to turn back any who tried to come and set foot on his land. The invaders had given a fairly good account of themselves, and blood had been shed on both sides. But they had been forced back across the river, leaving some of their number behind—men who, as had been promised them, could get a plot of ground six feet by three which would be their own forever.

Another wagon was coming down the street now, carrying more wounded. As the news spread, Fortymile boiled with anger. This was not the sort of thing they had counted on. It was bloody and bitter, and rage mounted to a dangerous point. Cliff Vaughan appeared, and was instantly surrounded by an angry crowd.

"You going to stand for this sort of thing, Sheriff?" someone demanded. "Murder and ambush?"

Vaughan faced them, his face cool and expressionless. Watching him, Stumpy had a feeling that the sheriff was secretly pleased at the outcome. After all, he had been a cattleman, and he was rather enjoying a victory for that side.

"From what I hear," he said, "it was an armed invasion. Which is against the law, itself. If it was met with force, that's all that could be expected."

There was a storm of angry denunciation, which the sheriff listened to imperturbably.

"Ain't you going to anything about it?" was the demand.

"Do? What can I do?" Vaughan shrugged. "I—"

"You mean to say that you don't aim to lift a finger, when things like this happen? That you won't go up there, as the law? A fine sort of sheriff you are."

Cliff Vaughan's face hardened a little.

"Mister," he said, "you'll find it pays to keep a civil tongue in your head. In the first place, as I've pointed out, every man who rode up there today got just what he was askin' for, when he staged an armed invasion. In the second, my jurisdiction stops at the river. What happens to the north of it isn't my business. I've no authority to go up there and interfere."

"Then who the blazes does have? Who is sheriff up there?"

Vaughan shrugged again.

"North of Saddle River has been the border," he said. "There's been no law up there, except Mart Cloud's. Some day, I suppose, there will be law there. But there isn't now."

Protest as they might, there was nothing that they could do about it. Vaughan was in the right. He had no jurisdiction north of the river. And secretly, Stumpy judged, the sheriff was glad that he did not have. At no time would he have been pleased to clash with Mart Cloud, and still less under the present circumstances.

But the bloodshed of that battle had made feeling run high, and there would be more trouble now, inevitably. Stumpy went on and found the judge, turning the bail money over to him.

"I'll see to getting Masterson out right away," the Judge promised. "Providing you're sure that you want him out, Stumpy. The way things are going, right now, and as hotheaded as he is—maybe it would be better to leave him there a few days longer. Give him a chance to cool down some."

"I promised to get him out as soon as I could," Stumpy said soberly. Gloria would expect it. And Wolf should be grateful enough for being freed to work with them. Though there was something to what the judge said, beyond question.

On the other hand, if Masterson was kept in jail, with feeling running as high as it did, the Wagon Wheel crew might well come storming into town, intent on freeing him. Stumpy mentioned this, and Quayle nodded.

"There's something to that . . . Well, we seem to be in for bad times. This Bannack is a natural troublemaker, from all I hear. It would be better for the country if he hadn't shown up. He wants to push things too fast."

On the street again, Stumpy turned toward the jail. He wanted to see Masterson as he came out, have a talk with him, and the two of them could then head toward the Saddle as quickly as possible. If he could get his former boss out of town and safely on the Saddle, where Gloria and the cattle were, then things should work out. But if Masterson met some of the inflamed nesters first, he might be back in jail before he ever got out of town at all.

He reached the jail to find that Wolf Masterson had been released and was gone, a full quarter of an hour before.

"He headed for the livery stable, is all I know," the deputy there explained. "I took it he was anxious to get out of town."

Dusk was already settling. Still anxious, but partly relieved by the news, Stumpy headed for the stable as well. If Wolf would get out of town and head for the Saddle, things would work out all right. And with it already growing dark, maybe he wouldn't be recognized, to get into trouble while on his way.

The town still seethed with excitement. That gun-battle on the Longhorn had really touched off trouble, and Mart Cloud would find plenty more before he was through with it. Avoiding the little knots of men clustered at corners, Stumpy hurried on, conscious of the scowling glances cast at him as he passed. Almost overnight, Fortymile had become a city of strangers, instead of a town where he knew everybody and was hailed by most of them as a friend.

Now these outlanders, seeing his dress, knew him for a cowboy, but they didn't recognize him as Stumpy Garford. As a cowboy, he was of that class which they regarded instinctively as enemies.

He reached the stable, to find Whiskey Bill in charge, his nose like a beacon in the dimness of the huge barn. Whiskey Bill was never sober, but he could do the work of a roustabout around the stable.

"Wolf?" he asked. "Yeah, he come in here a spell ago and got a hawss—left a spell back. Plumb proddy, even for him."

"What was bothering him this time?" Stumpy asked.

"Seems he'd just heard how his cattle was being taken to yore spread, no'th of the river. And man, was he mad!" Whiskey Bill leaned forward confidentially, blowing a breath into Stumpy's face which nearly knocked him off his feet.

"Stumpy," he adjured, "I'm drunk—I'm alwaysh drunk. You know that. But jus' the same, take my advice an' k-keep away from that hombre. He's plumb poison."

"Why?" Stumpy was surprised. "He's not mad at me, is he?"

"If he ain't, he give a gol-durn good imitation o' bein'. Said that damn Garford was a cattle-thief, and swore he'd shoot yuh on sight! And then he went out of here like a bat out of hell!"

It was plain enough that Wolf Masterson did not know that it was Stumpy who had raised his bail and freed him from behind the bars. Evidently he had given scant thought as to why he was being released in the first place. Always headstrong, his already inflamed thoughts had been further wrought up by the news he had somehow heard, that his herd was being driven to his former employee's new ranch.

Masterson had jumped immediately to the conclusion that, in taking them away from the Wagon Wheel, Stumpy was trying to steal them. And now he was acting accordingly.

Probably the information had been twisted in transmission, and just what he had heard there could be no telling. But the damage had already been done. Grim-faced, Stumpy secured his own horse and set out for home.

It was late when he reached the river. The camp on the south side showed where some of the nesters were still waiting, after their futile sortie across the river that morning. The scene of that bloody foray had been off on Longhorn land, and all was quiet and peaceful enough now. Stumpy gave the camp a wide berth, and reached his own place after midnight.

But he had seen the Wagon Wheel cattle, bedded down in good grass, weary and contented after their long drive, but safely home. That represented a definite victory. Once Masterson understood the situation, he would probably be reasonable.

Morning, however, was not so encouraging. Gloria was there, and her presence, here on his own ranch, compensated for a lot of the rest. But her father had not appeared, though he had left Fortymile ahead of Stumpy.

Gloria looked about with kindling eyes. The big house was far enough along now to be habitable, the other buildings were also making a good showing. The place that Stumpy had chosen was a natural setting for a ranch home, and this morning the sun was shining, red and yellow leaves splashed the landscape with color.

"It's a beautiful country, Stumpy," Gloria said enthusiastically. "I never saw a finer place than this is going to be."

"Like it?" Stumpy's eyes warmed. "I hoped you would, Gloria. I was thinking of you when I picked this spot."

She glanced swiftly at him and away again, color staining her cheeks.

"That was nice of you," she agreed. "Did—did you get Dad out yesterday—or wouldn't they let him go?"

"He's out," Stumpy said. "I raised his bail money. But I didn't get to talk to him. I kind of got held up, and time I reached the jail, he was gone. I had sort of supposed that he'd be here, before this."

"Maybe he went back to—to the Wagon Wheel." Her eyes were shining, but her lips trembled a little. "I knew you would do it, Stumpy. But tell me. How much was the bail?"

"Five thousand."

Gloria stared at him in amazement—surprised that it should be so high in the first place, and bewildered that he could swing such a deal, along with all the other expenses he had had of late.

"That's a lot of money," she commented gravely. "But we'll pay you back, of course. Thanks a lot, Stumpy."

"There's no reason why it needs to be paid back," Stumpy grinned. "Judge Quayle has fixed his hearing for tomorrow afternoon, and maybe we can clear the whole thing up then. If we can, I'll get my money back, and it will be all settled."

"Oh, I hope so." Her eyes were shining again. "I feel as if this was a new beginning, Stumpy—a grand and glorious beginning."

"We'll sure aim to make it so," he agreed. "Makes me feel pretty fine, too, havin' you for a partner."

She stuck out her hand, man-fashion.

"Shake, partner." Her voice was a little husky. "We'll make a go of it, won't we?"

"We sure will," Stumpy agreed. "Let's go have some breakfast, before those other fellows eat it all."

Breakfast was a gay affair, in the newly built dining room, a long, shed-like affair adjoining the cook shack. The two crews, Wagon Wheel and Saddle, were working together as one today, and both were elated at this latest turn of events. The Saddle boys, because they were glad to see cattle on the heretofore vacant land, and the Wagon Wheel, who up to a day or so ago had been desperate, not knowing which way to turn. To all of them, it seemed like an ideal solution of the problem. Stumpy's former fellow-riders looked upon him with a new respect.

Stumpy issued orders, taking every precaution to guard against surprise. For a moment, it was probable that Mart Cloud would have his hands full with the nesters, but Stumpy was taking no chances on a sudden foray of any sort. This was his land now, to have and to hold—and he aimed to hold it.

At mid-forenoon, increasingly uneasy because there was still no sign of Wolf Masterson, Stumpy and Gloria rode out to have a look at the cattle. Stumpy had said nothing of what had happened the night before, or of Masterson's threat. But this continued absence smelled of trouble.

They found the herd, lazily contented today, spread out in a low sweeping valley below them, and paused to feast their eyes on them. Stumpy loved good cattle, and so did Gloria. And these Wagon Wheel beeves were among the best in the country.

Wolf Masterson was a good stockman. He had started, a quarter of a century before, with the same sort of stock as had all his neighbors—long-horned, bony cattle, slightly better in grade than the original Texas longhorns which had first been driven up the long trails. But that stock of twenty-five years ago could scarcely be recognized in these cattle today.

Masterson had consistently built up his herd with Hereford blood, until now they were equally hardy, but these steers would weigh more than twice what their ancestors had weighed, and it was good, solid flesh, not bone and horn. They represented the best blood in the Saddle River country, and were easily the finest herd.

They sat to watch a minute, and Chinook, off some distance, saw them and galloped up. There was a dogged, worried look on his homely face.

"I just heard some news, Stumpy, and it ain't so good," he blurted out. "Know where Wolf went, last night? He headed for the Longhorn, and bedded there."

"Probably didn't know just where to go, the way everything's been lately," Stumpy said easily. "And he's always been a good friend of Cloud's."

"Who told you, Chinook?" Gloria demanded.

"One of the Longhorn riders," Chinook explained. "He was out, kind of scoutin' around, looked like, and I surprised him, come out on him 'fore he had a chance to cut and run.

It was Bill Sterns, and we always got along pretty good, so he give me the news. He says Wolf is out gunnin' for you, Stumpy. Claimin' that yuh stole his herd."

Gloria's face went white, and Stumpy wished heartily for a chance to kick his over-zealous but blundering foreman, but there had been no chance to stop him.

"Why—he can't do that," Gloria protested. "How can he think of such a thing?"

"Dunno." Chinook shook his head. "I'm right sorry, Miss Gloria, but yuh know how Wolf is—he gets ideas, and sometimes they ain't quite correct. Anyway, that's what Bill was tellin' me. And I thought yuh ought to know."

He swung off at a trot again, and they sat for a minute in silence. There was little that could be said.

"It's Mart Cloud," Gloria exclaimed suddenly. "He hates you, Stumpy, and he's been telling Dad a lot of lies. It's too bad that Dad rode that way, but of course he didn't know."

Masterson had known, as Stumpy knew, but he still agreed with her. Cloud had probably fed the fires of Wolf's anger in every way he knew how.

They were silent a while, and then, as they watched, a rider broke out of a patch of brush about a quarter of a mile away. Wolf Masterson himself.

From where he rode, he could see part of the big herd of grazing cattle, but it was doubtful if any of the watchers of the herd had seen him yet. Nor had he sighted Gloria or Stumpy.

"There he is!" Gloria exclaimed. "And he's alone, thank goodness. I'll go and talk to him. You keep out of sight, Stumpy, till I've explained things to him."

"Just as you say," Stumpy agreed, and watched her ride at a fast trot to join her father. For a minute, Wolf did not see her. Then he heard the sound of an approaching horse, and whirled, hand dropping toward his holstered gun. Seeing Gloria, he relaxed a little and waited, but he did not ride to meet her, and he maintained a forbidding silence.

Stumpy circled swiftly, keeping out of sight, riding to where he could see and hear what went on, while still hidden by some trees. If anybody could make the old rannyhan see straight, it was Gloria, but in Wolf's present mood, Stumpy was doubtful if even she could do it.

"Dad!" Gloria exclaimed. "I'm so glad to see you!"

"Then what the blazes are you doing on land that's supposed to be Stumpy Garford's?" Wolf demanded, and his voice quivered with pent-up rage. At his tone, as much as his words, Gloria stopped suddenly, the light going out of her eyes, cheeks whitening. Without giving her a chance to answer, Wolf talked on, pouring out his vials of wrath.

"You don't need to tell me. I know how you've been hoodwinked, takin' my cattle up here, helping him steal them. Though I did suppose that any daughter of mine would have more pride than to take up with any damned nester, after what the nesters have just done to us. More pride than to sleep and eat on a ranch of that sort, or to help a nester to steal from us!"

"Why—why, Dad, you don't understand—" Gloria said breathlessly.

"Don't understand, eh?" Wolf roared. "I understand only too well. And I won't have it. Nesters!" He spat out the word, tense with venom.

"But Stumpy's no nester," Gloria exclaimed. "He's a cattleman—"

"He's a cattle-thief, that's what he is. No nester? Didn't he come in here and grab a lot of Cloud's spread, homesteadin' it just like all the rest, but with a big crew of gunmen to back him up? Stealin' just like all the lousy squatters, to smash all our outfits. He's been hand in glove with all of them from the start, helpin' them when Cloud tried to stop them from takin' the rest of his range. Thank goodness I've found you. I've come to take you and the cattle home."

"But we can't go home, Dad. Every foot of our land is taken—"

"Don't I know it?" he shouted. "That's what the nesters do to honest cattlemen! But I'm taking you home, just the same. To the only home we've got left, with another honest cattleman, who's got the nerve to fight for what belongs to him! And I'll fight with him till every nester is run out of this country, or I'm killed! Come on. The Longhorn's your home, from now on."

"Not that, Dad. Mart Cloud is a murderer—"

"A murderer?" Wolf's face was terrible as his voice. "A murderer, because he fights to protect his own? I suppose I'm a murderer too, then. Because I'm standin' with Mart Cloud, come hell or high water. You've been listenin' to that mealy-mouthed Garford, the dirty, sneakin' traitor—"

A dangerous red was creeping into Gloria's cheeks now. She was not Wolf Masterson's daughter for nothing.

"Stumpy Garford is no traitor! I won't listen to such things about him—"

"You'll listen to what I say—"

"I won't listen to such things about Stumpy! He had me bring the cattle here because—"

"He had you bring them here so he could steal them—"

"—Because there was nowhere else to take them, and he offered me his pasture. Then, because I asked him to, he got you out of prison, paying your bail—"

Masterson wasn't listening. It was probable that he had not even heard what she said about prison and bail, for he was trying, and with good success, to outshout her.

"I tell you he's a cattle-thief, a nester, a sneakin' double-crosser, a traitor—"

He raved on, naming Stumpy almost everything he could lay his tongue to. Stumpy had seen him in rages before, but never such a towering passion as this. White-faced again, Gloria had grown quiet, waiting for the tirade to spend itself. As abruptly as he had begun, Masterson quieted too, an ominous calmness.

"You're to come home with me, Gloria," he said. "Here and now. I won't have a daughter of mine stayin' on the same place with a skunk like him."

Gloria stared back at him, her mouth twisting a little, like a small child about to cry. But her voice was cold, steady.

"I'm sorry, Dad. Sorry that you feel that way. But I'm staying here—with the cattle."

"I'm takin' the cattle, too."

"I don't think so."

Masterson stared for a moment, incredulous. His face reddened again, but there was no explosion.

"As your father, I'm tellin' you to come home. And this is the last time I'll ask you. You'll come now—or never !"

CHAPTER 13

AGAIN, FOR a moment, Gloria's lips quivered. Stumpy, watching helplessly, knew what a struggle this was for her, what her decision was costing her. But she had as determined a will as her father, and when she was convinced that she was right, nothing could swerve her.

"I'm sorry, Father. I wish you'd just listen to—"

"Listen to the lies that cattle-thief's been telling you?" Masterson shouted. "I've heard too many of them already. You're no daughter of mine. You've made your bed—now lie in it! I'm takin' the cattle, right soon—takin' them at gunpoint if necessary. Tell your precious Stumpy that. And better tell him to keep out of my way, for if he ever gets lined in my gun-lights, there'll be one less nester in this country!"

He jerked his horse around, spurring savagely, heading back for the Longhorn. Stumpy watched him go. There was nothing else to do. No need to try and stop him and make him listen to reason. That would only invite gun-play, as Wolf had threatened.

He turned as Masterson rode out of sight, and joined Gloria, still sitting her horse, a woe-begone, desolate little figure now, unmoving until he reached her. Two tears trickled slowly from under her nearly closed eyelids, splashed down her cheeks. Stumpy slid off his horse and stood beside her, reaching up his arms, and she slipped from the saddle and into them, collapsing in a storm of tears.

Stumpy held her, saying nothing, waiting until she had quieted a little. Finally she lifted a drenched face toward him.

"I couldn't do anything else, could I, Stumpy? He's wrong —utterly, completely wrong, and Mart Cloud is just using him to make things worse. I couldn't go back there—not to Cloud's place."

"Of course you couldn't," Stumpy agreed. "Your home is right here on the Saddle, Gloria."

She was silent a minute, her eyes troubled.

"Even if I had gone back with him, I couldn't make him see things any differently," she said hopelessly. "But, oh, Stumpy!" her voice was a wail. "Things are such a mess!"

"They sure are," Stumpy agreed again. "But as the old sayin' has it, it's always darkest just before it starts to get light again. They'll work out."

"I know that you're doing the right thing, Stumpy. Your way is the only way that can save things, for any of us. You are getting hold of this land, so that we'll have a legal title to it, and that's the only way that a cattleman can continue to exist at all, in this country. All the other land is going to be taken—even Mart Cloud can't stop them, no matter how much he fights. The law, the federal government, are against him, and that's too big a combination—and the homesteaders are so thick that they'd beat him anyway."

"You're right there," Stumpy agreed. "The country's changing, and people have to change with it, or go under."

"And Mart Cloud is a murderer," she went on. "Blowing up that dam to flood the river and trap those women and children, without any warning—that was plain murder. And letting the nesters come onto his last yesterday, and ride into an ambush before he challenged them, then shooting them down—that was plain murder, too. I couldn't go over there, Stumpy—I just couldn't."

She wiped her eyes and smiled up at him, a ghost of a smile which twisted his heart, then swung lithely into the saddle again.

"I don't know just what we're going to do about a lot of things," she confessed. "But I do trust you, Stumpy. And we're partners."

"We sure are," Stumpy agreed heartily. "And I'll aim to be worthy of that trust, Gloria."

He wanted to say more—to tell her that he loved her, that he was ready to marry her and give her a home and the full measure of his protection, then and there. But it wouldn't be fair to say such things, not right then. He sensed that she understood, and for the time it was better to let it go at that. He couldn't say anything more, not after that bitter interview which she had just had with her father.

The misguided old rannyhan! Somehow, some way, he had to convince Wolf of what a mistake he was making, get him to see the light. Once that was done, and he was reconciled with Gloria again, it would be time to tell Gloria how he felt. Stumpy cursed under his breath. If Hankins had just left him alone, the day before, kept his gratitude to himself for a spell longer, so that he could have reached the jail and Wolf's ear before he was turned loose!

"Stumpy." Gloria's voice was troubled again. "You heard what he said—about shooting you, if he got a chance?"

"I heard," Stumpy agreed. He didn't try to comfort her by saying that likely Wolf hadn't meant all he said. Stumpy knew better, and so did Gloria. Unlike many men, who say wild things in the heat of passion, without meaning them, Wolf Masterson always meant what he said, no matter how wild.

"You'll have to keep away from him, Stumpy—until he's had a chance to change his mind."

"Reckon you're right there," Stumpy conceded.

"But—but if you should meet him, Stumpy—" her lips were trembling again. "Promise me that you—that you won't use a gun. Please!"

"Of course I won't," Stumpy agreed. "I wouldn't shoot your Dad, Gloria."

Abruptly, she swerved her horse toward him, her head was on his chest for a moment. When she lifted it, her eyes were shining, but she was blinking back the tears at the same time.

"You're just the finest man I ever knew, Stumpy," she whispered. "And maybe I'm terribly selfish. Maybe I'm asking you to stand still and be—be murdered!"

They returned to the house, and Stumpy set about fixing up a room for Gloria to occupy, to have for her own, until the rest of the house should be made habitable. He would continue to bunk out with the rest of the boys, of course.

One of his first acts was to dispatch one of the men with a team and wagon to Fortymile. He could bring back a load of stuff for Gloria, who had lost everything she had when the Wagon Wheel was overrun. More to the point, he was to bring back Mrs. Luke, who had been housekeeper on the Wagon Wheel for the last several years.

Mrs. Luke had gone to Fortymile when evicted from the Wagon Wheel, gone under protest but at Gloria's orders, until other arrangements could be made. She was an excellent housekeeper, sharp-tongued and capable, but she had been like a mother to Gloria, and Stumpy intended to see her installed in her old capacity at the Saddle, as soon as possible. Gloria rewarded him with a smile.

"You're awfully good to me, Stumpy," she said.

"We're partners, aren't we?" Stumpy demanded.

He could still smile, but off by himself, he had no inclination to mirth. He had warned the men to be doubly on the lookout for trouble, though he had an idea that, for the moment, Mart Cloud would be too fully occupied with other troubles to back Masterson's play and send his crew to try and take the herd. For the advantage lay with Stumpy, in that the Wagon Wheel crew were working for Stumpy now, and then would do as Gloria told them.

Later, of course, Cloud would probably try it—but there was no hurry, even from his viewpoint.

Even without an attack coming immediately, there was plenty else for Stumpy to worry about now. To send a messenger to Wolf Masterson and try to explain things, to get him to be reasonable, was so foolhardy as not even to be thought of, after he had refused to listen to his own daughter.

And it was equally out of the question for Stumpy to go and try and see Wolf himself, at the present time. It could only lead to more trouble, and do no good.

But while Wolf Masterson sulked on the Longhorn and nursed his grouch, time was running out, both for himself and for Stumpy. It was apparent, from what Wolf had said, that he did not know that Stumpy had raised the money for his bail. And he hadn't heard when Gloria had tried to tell him. If he had known, his attitude would have been different, because of his fierce pride.

Since he didn't know it, it was unlikely that he would learn the truth over at the Longhorn. Worse still, if he did find out at this stage of the game, he'd probably be just cantankerous enough to jump his bail, on the assumption that Stumpy had figured to buy his beef herd at such a price.

The day ended with no new disturbance, and no more news of any clashes, anywhere on the range. And the next day dawned as sunny and full of promise as the one before—full of promise of trouble.

By evening, Stumpy knew that the trouble was real enough for Wolf and himself, but in different ways. He had seen no way of staving off this latest disaster, and a messenger, riding back from town, had confirmed his worst fears.

Wolf Masterson was an outlaw now. He had known that his hearing was to be that afternoon, and had deliberately stayed away from it, forfeiting his bail. Now he still had the same charges against him, and was a fugitive from justice.

That was bad. About equally bad, from Stumpy's point of view, was the fact that it was his money that Wolf had forfeited. Stumpy had expected to get it back. Now it was gone, past all hope of recovery. And he was broke—flat broke.

Chinook wandered in to where he sat.

"Just thought I'd remind yuh, Stumpy," he nodded. "To-morrow's pay-day for the boys, you know."

Stumpy ate breakfast with the boys, his face impassive as usual. After breakfast was the usual time for paying up. Nine out of ten of them, knowing that they couldn't get to town under these circumstances, would hand their wages back to him until a more convenient time. But he'd have to tell them, in another ten minutes, that he couldn't pay them today, probably not for a month. He knew about how these boys would take it, but when the news got out, Mart Cloud and Tom Bannack would know how to take advantage of such a situation.

"Whoa, gol-durn ye! Don't roll that wall-eye up at me and look mistreated! Ye've durn near shook every piece of meat off a me frame as it is. I—"

"Baldy!" Stumpy gave a yell and was out of the door, grabbing the hand of his partner, who was laboriously dis-mounting from the saddle of a dejected-looking cayuse. Baldy gave a whoop in return and shook hands as though he hadn't seen Stumpy for at least ten years. He was a roly-poly little man of indefinite age, with a perpetual twinkle in his eye and head as bald as an egg, and a hugely ferocious mustache beneath it.

"How'd you get here so soon?" Stumpy demanded. "I didn't suppose you could make it."

"And why not?" Baldy demanded, rubbing himself tenderly. "I been ridin' out from Fortymile dang near all night, and I won't be able tuh set down for a week. But yuh sent that tellygram, sayin' to come a-runnin', and I been travelin' steady since then. Breakfast ready?"

"Sure is, Old-Timer. Come in and fill up."

That, Baldy proceeded to do without delay, stowing away a prodigious amount of food. Stumpy watched him admiringly. The message must have got through without delay, and as Baldy said, he had certainly lost no time in coming on the run.

The cowboys had all left the dining room by now, pushing back their chairs and going off with instinctive delicacy to leave the boss alone with his guest. Such mundane matters as pay could wait until they'd had their confab undisturbed.

Baldy sighed with repletion, and turned.

"What's troublin' yuh, Stumpy?" he asked. "Somethin' go wrong? Swaller an egg and have it peep? Looks tuh me like yuh was swingin' a right ambitious deal here, for a cowpuncher. Tell me about it."

Stumpy did, starting at the beginning, for Baldy had known little of what went on up there. He listened with respectful attention and no interruptions, as became a man of the desert, who could go for days or weeks without hearing another human voice.

"Sounds like a good idea," he nodded finally. "And so this Wolf goes wild, eh, and gets away with all yore ready cash. That it?"

"That's about the size of it," Stumpy confessed. "Looks like I kind of pulled a boner there, but it seemed like the best idea at the time."

"Reckon I'd of done the same," Baldy nodded comfortably. "Well, I come prepared. Have somebody bring in my saddle-bags. They're bulgin' with money."

Stumpy stepped to the door and brought the saddle-bags himself. Baldy up-ended them on the table, pouring out money—gold coin and bills.

"Five thousand dollars," he nodded carelessly. "Didn't know how much yuh might be a needin', Stumpy, but I guess I hit it about right."

"You sure did, Baldy." Stumpy's voice was a little hoarse. "It's a life-saver. I'll give you my half-interest in the mine for it, if that's all right."

"Well, it ain't, gol-durn yore ornery hide!" Baldy bounded to his feet like a rubber ball. "Of all the cow-kicked, knock-kneed, no-good, low-down, ornery, cantankerous, spavin-jointed and worthless suns-uh-guns I ever met up with in my whole c'reer, I reckon yuh get the potato medal! Ain't we partners, gol-durn it? Ain't I got money in both fists, and more comin' in till I don't know what tuh do with the durn stuff? Besides, I'd never of had a cent of it if it hadn't been for you, grab-stakin' me all them years, when yuh didn't figger to get anything back. Want tuh insult me? Take the money. If you want to pay it back out of what keeps comin', yuh can, though it don't make a dang bit uh diff'rence. But don't go gettin' insultin' around here no more!"

Stumpy would have weathered that storm, with a crew of the sort which he now had behind him, one way or another. But it helped a lot to have a partner like Baldy.

Work was going forward rapidly on the buildings, getting them ready before winter should clamp down. Meanwhile there was a lull in trouble, a welcome breathing spell. Wolf Masterson had declared that he was coming to take his cattle, but he could do that now only when his host was ready to ride with him, crew and all. And for the moment, Mart Cloud was busy with other things, too—chiefly the threat of nesters who were constantly pressing on the borders of the Longhorn.

But that both Cloud and Masterson would be anxious to strike, when they deemed the time opportune, there was no question. Stumpy and Gloria discussed the matter of the herd.

"After all, they're his cattle," Gloria said soberly. "At least, Dad owns a half-interest in the herd—more than any-one else. And that gives him a legal right to take them, if he wants to."

Stumpy was surprised. He had long known that Gloria's mother had had a good deal of money, which she had put into the Wagon Wheel. And because of that circumstance, a two-fifths interest in the herd had been in Gloria's name for the last few years. But he had taken it for granted that Wolf himself held the other three-fifths.

"Who owns the other tenth?" he asked.

"Curt Tucker," Gloria explained. "Dad was pretty hard up, here, a couple of years back, and Tucker loaned him the money, and took an interest in the herd in return."

That was all news to Stumpy. But it put a new complexion on things. However, the main point was still unchanged. Wolf Masterson was the largest owner of the herd, and if he insisted on taking them, right was on his side. Rather than have a gun-battle, Stumpy was willing to let him take the stock, when he came after them.

To do so would upset all Stumpy's calculations, but if he refused, he would be stepping outside the law, and becoming what Masterson had called him—a cattle thief. He smiled wryly and went on with his work. It was right-down funny, when you stopped to think about it, how a girl like Gloria could have a father like Wolf Masterson. Though Wolf wouldn't be so bad if he'd use his head a little.

Baldy had remained on the Saddle for nearly a week, keenly interested in all that went on, hopeful that trouble would flame forth afresh so that he could take a hand in it. When nothing happened, and he had seen all there was to see, he lost interest and prepared to return to his old stamping grounds. Stumpy drove him to Fortymile in a spring wagon, which, as Baldy declared, was a lot more comfortable and civilized way of travel than for a man to make a clothespin of himself over a cayuse, and try to split himself to pieces.

"And which it wouldn't take much more for me tuh do just that," Baldy sighed. "I get along fine with a burro, but he's built diff'rent, and has a nobler outlook on life. These here cayuses, they're a plumb ornery breed."

Stumpy didn't argue with him. He preferred a cayuse any day to a burro, and this life to prospecting, but it was every man to his own taste, and if it hadn't been for Baldy and his quest for gold, the Saddle would still have been a dream. Baldy's prompt response to his wire had been a life-saver.

They swung into town, the horses' hoofs kicking up plops of dust on the main street. Once more, Stumpy was struck by the change in the town. Fortymile had pretty well made the transition. It was no longer a cow town. And today, as on the occasion of his previous visit, it seemed to seethe with excitement.

"What's been happenin' now?" Stumpy asked an acquaintance.

"Ain't you heard, livin' right there side of it? Seems like you'd be the first to know."

"Nary word," Stumpy confessed. "But you want to remember that it's a big country up there. And when we stay home and mind our business, we're a long way from anywhere."

"I'd think you'd want to be. With Cloud and Masterson for neighbors."

"They been cuttin' up again?"

"Plenty, I'd say. There was a clash last night. Seems about a dozen of the nesters done a sneak across the river, under cover of dark, a few nights back, and kind of looked over the land. Then they come in to town here and filed on 'em, all legal. Sort of stole a march on Cloud that time."

"Sounds so. By the way, hasn't Cloud or any of his men filed on some of that land?"

"Nary acre." Stumpy's friend grinned. "It's all over the country, how yuh advised Cloud to folley yore lead and file on his own land, to hold it. And danged good advice, I'd say. But he's sworn that he's had that land for years, and that it belongs to him without no more didoes, and that according, he'll hold it without any more foolin'. Bitin' off his nose to spite his face, I'd say. Likely he would have filed, if anybody but you had suggested it to him."

Stumpy nodded. The overweening pride of such men as Masterson and Cloud was leading them straight to certain downfall.

"You were sayin' something about last night?" he suggested.

"Oh, yes. Well, last night the nesters come back, with their papers, to take over their land. Bannack was leadin' them. There was a battle, and Cloud drove 'em back across the river—all but three or four, who won't be interested in homesteads no more."

"So that's what the excitement is about today, eh?"

"Mostly. It's bigger'n that, though. Folks has been kind of het up about things for quite a spell—like Wolf Masterson jumpin' his bail and holin' up with Cloud. And then last night, Cloud hit from ambush again, shootin' without warning. Which makes about the third time, and it's plain murder, of course. Main mistake they made last night, was that them homesteaders had legal papers, and so was backed by Uncle Sam. Cloud was tryin' to run 'em off their own land. And so, today, there are Federal men on their way, going in after Cloud and Masterson, on murder warrants."

A cold wind seemed to blow on Stumpy, the sun had lost its warmth. This was what he had been afraid of—open outlawry for Wolf Masterson. His friend was relating details with gusto.

"I reckon you won't have to worry about them being neighbors of yore's much longer, Stumpy. The law'll clean 'em out proper this time. They're aimin' tuh take 'em dead or alive, then confiscate their property, or at least tie it up, to make a settlement for all who claim damages against Cloud or Masterson, and that's a plenty. They'll take the land, which ain't theirs tuh begin with, and every last head

of stock, too. When they get through, there won't be no
more Longhorn than they is Wagon Wheel now."

CHAPTER 14

GLORIA'S FACE had whitened at the news. She followed
Stumpy into a room which had been fixed up as an office, and
sank down on an arm of his chair.

"So Dad is called an outlaw now," she said dully. "I—I
was hoping, somehow, that it wouldn't get that bad."

Stumpy nodded. He had told her that much, omitting the
worse news that the law would be coming after Masterson
on a charge of murder.

"It listens pretty bad," Stumpy conceded. "But maybe
things will turn out better than they look. I—"

There was a knock on the door, and Chinook came in.

"Just got a little news, that I figgered you'd want to
know," he explained. "I'm payin' one of Cloud's men to tip
us off—and he says they're getting set to come over here and
take the cattle, likely in the morning. They're countin' on a
battle, but they're ready for it."

Stumpy and Gloria looked at each other, after Chinook
had departed. The news, in a way, was logical enough. With
showdown fast approaching, Cloud and Masterson aimed
to move fast, to get control of everything and wipe out opposition with a ruthless hand. It amounted to that.

"If he only knew that we don't aim to give him any trouble, that way," Gloria whispered.

"But maybe we will," Stumpy sighed. "Things have
changed, lately." He explained what the law intended to do
—to take over all property which belonged to Cloud and
Masterson, to hold against settlement of claims made against
them.

That would mean that every man who had been shot,
either killed or wounded in the clashes so far, on either
ranch, could put in, directly or through relatives, a claim
for damages. It was the law of the east, of old settled country, transplanted along with other innovations to this new
land where such things had been unheard-of, up to now.

But that it would stick, there was small doubt. And once
claims had been settled, there would be nothing left of
either outfit.

"The way it looks to me, it's up to us to hold the cattle," Stumpy said. "For several reasons, and your father's sake as well as our own. If they take them, then the law will get hold of them—and when they finish, there'll be nothing left, either for you or Wolf. Whereas if we hold them here, the law can't touch 'em—and while maybe some of these claims that'll be plastered on are honest, there'll be a whole lot which are just plain graft. And I figure that we've a better right than they have."

"But can we hold them legally?" Gloria asked.

Stumpy nodded.

"If we keep them here on Saddle land, we can," he agreed. "I stopped in and had a talk with Curt Tucker, and explained the situation to him. Fact is, I bought half of his interest in the herd, myself. So, while it's a small one, I've got a legal interest in them now."

Gloria tried to smile at him, though it was a wan attempt.

"You had that before, Stumpy, as long as I have any interest in them," she said.

"I know," he nodded. "And I was thinking of your share, Gloria. If the law grabbed them, your share and mine and Curt's, all being minor interests, wouldn't get far—not with the way public opinion's runnin' in this country these days. But Curt, he agrees with us. So we're holdin' the stock, and between us, we have a half-interest in the herd. And that gives us a legal control over the other half-interest, since your father is counted an outlaw, and can't legally handle it while that holds. So, for his protection as well as our own, we'll hold on to them. And the law can't come onto the Saddle to touch them."

"It sounds like the only thing to do," Gloria agreed. "But, oh, Stumpy, all this has nearly worried me sick. And if they do come in the morning—" she shivered.

"I'm hopin' they won't come in the morning," Stumpy said slowly. "Maybe, if I could get Wolf to see reason—"

"How could you do that?"

Stumpy grinned faintly.

"Only way I can figure out, is by talkin' to him. But if he knew what the real situation was—well, he's hot-headed, but he's never been accused of being a fool, even by his worst enemies."

"But it's so dangerous, Stumpy. You'd have to go over

on to the Longhorn to see him—and he's sworn to shoot you
on sight—"

"It's either have a try at it, or have him shootin' at me
on sight in the morning, with the rest of Cloud's crew doing
the same," Stumpy reminded. "And they've gathered a big
crew, a lot of them professional gunmen. I'll be careful,
don't worry about that."

Gloria was dubious and troubled, but she gave her con-
sent. Leaving his gun at home, as he had promised her to
do long since, Stumpy saddled a horse and set out as darkness was closing down. It was a black night, with lowering
clouds, and a decided bite to the air. The ground was still
bare of snow, however, partly frozen.

Stumpy was under no illusions as to the difficulty of the
job he had tackled. Wolf was living on the Longhorn, and
added to his own natural irascibility and hot-headedness, he
had come directly under the influence of Mart Cloud.

And Cloud was never hot-headed. He might lose his temper, but he never lost his head. He was a cold-blooded
schemer, and he had proven himself utterly ruthless. Moreover, he had moved cleverly to bring Masterson under his
control, to get him in the same boat. Cloud would shoot from
ambush, commit murder without compunction. Wolf Masterson wasn't that sort of a man at all, and probably he had
had no direct hand in what had taken place. But Cloud had
gotten him in with him, even to the responsibility. Cloud
wanted him, because Masterson, like himself, was an enemy
of Stumpy Garford.

And when all the rest was cleared up, here north of the
river, Cloud planned on a full and final settlement with
Stumpy. All the rest was trifling, compared to that. But
he was a man to take his time, to plan well and strike hard.
And if he could find Stumpy on his land, he'd be ready for a
quick and final settlement. The mere fact that Stumpy was
unarmed would merely seem like a piece of good luck to him.

As he approached the buildings of the Longhorn, Stumpy
moved cautiously. Lights glowed in several windows, from
the cook shack, the bunkhouse and at least two or three other
buildings. There was a certain constant watchfulness here
on the Longhorn which was ill-suited to his purpose, a
watchfulness induced by the threat of the homesteaders and
the law alike.

Stumpy tied his horse off at some distance, in a clump of choke-cherry brush, half-denuded of leaves now by the whispering winds. Going on foot, moving like a shadow, he came to a rear window of the bunkhouse, standing partly open to allow some of the smoke to drift out.

The room was full of men. Ordinarily, at this hour of the evening, they would have been playing poker or some such pursuit. Now, several of them were cleaning guns or engaged in similar grim preparations, and all of them giving an ear to what Mart Cloud himself was saying.

"So that's the size of it," he said, biting off the words. "In the morning we're ridin' for the Saddle—as Garford calls it. We're going in force, every man of us, and we're bringing back the Wagon Wheel herd."

He nodded, turned and went out. The crew exchanged significant glances, and went on wordlessly about the job which had been engrossing them, one or two whistling thoughtfully. Wolf Masterson was not in the room. Satisfied of that, Stumpy moved away, paused. Cloud and Masterson were standing on the front porch of Cloud's house, talking.

"Everything's set," Cloud said. "We'll get what belongs to you back tomorrow, Wolf."

"That's fine," Masterson growled. "Well, I'm going to turn in and get some sleep. See you in the morning, Mart."

He moved off in the darkness, heading for a smaller cabin, standing a little apart from the others, where a light glowed. Stumpy followed. Here was the break he had been hoping for, a chance to get to Masterson, alone. Now, if he could make him listen, then there would be a good chance of making him listen to reason as well.

Wolf Masterson opened the door, and the reflected light showed Stumpy that the room was empty otherwise. He stuck his foot forward, preventing the door from closing, and Masterson swung quickly, startled.

"Evenin', Wolf," Stumpy said casually. "I'd like a word with you—"

CHAPTER 15

THAT WAS as far as he got. Stumpy had intended that, in the next breath, he would make it plain that he wanted only a friendly talk, but it was apparent that events of the past few weeks had put Masterson's always taut nerves very much on edge. He moved with bewildering speed, and a gun seemed to flow into his hand by magic, to be thrust close into Stumpy's face, and, never a man to subdue his voice, Masterson was fairly yelling back at him.

"So you want a word with me, do you? Well, damn you, Garford, I'm the one that'll be havin' the word, all the words there are—"

The crash of a gun blasted loud on the night, from off toward the bunkhouse. At the same instant Stumpy felt a tug at the hair at the back of his head, massed and crowded down there by his hat. It was as though somebody had given it a sudden vicious jerk, and it didn't need the prickling, stinging sensation of his skin to know that the bullet had grazed past there, cutting through the hair, barely breaking the skin. A bullet aimed to smash clear through his head and kill him as he stood.

Wolf Masterson was fully as surprised as Stumpy himself, and nearly as displeased. But he was a man to think and act swiftly, whatever he did, and now he moved without a second's hesitation. One hand reached out to shove Stumpy violently to one side, saving his life as a second bullet whistled past. And Masterson, whipped to a towering rage, did not wait for a third.

"Stop it!" he roared. "You low-down, murderin' hound. Stop it, or I'll fill you full of lead myself. Of all the sneakin' skunk tricks—"

For a few moments he went on to relieve his mind, with a vocabulary that left little to the imagination, pouring out his wrath upon the killer who, recognizing Stumpy, had thus tried to murder him from ambush.

The realization that events were moving at a gallop jerked Masterson away from that theme to more practical matters. Stumpy had crouched there in the deep shadow of the building for a moment, tremendously relieved at Masterson's latest reaction. The swiftness of the cattleman's change had lifted a big load off his mind. Whatever else Wolf Masterson was, he was no killer, and he had proved it.

Anxiety over the same notion diverted Masterson's tirade against the gunman, to swift explanation.

"The damn skunk," he growled. "I ain't got as low as murder—not yet! But as for you, Garford, get to the devil out of here and stay—I'm comin' for my cattle in the mornin', come hell or high water, and no holds barred."

His advice, to get out of there, was excellent. There was no possible chance now to talk to him, as Stumpy had hoped for. Attracted by the shooting and shouting, the others were pouring out of the bunkhouse now, and unless he made his getaway in a hurry, he wouldn't make it at all. And if he was captured—well, there were plenty in that crew who, like their employer, weren't squeamish. They wouldn't bother with capturing him.

Angered by the cowardly attempt at murdering Stumpy while he was talking to him, Masterson was making no attempt to stop him now. That had been a bit too much for him to swallow. But neither was he making any attempt to stop the others. Stumpy ran, thankful for the deep darkness, feeling a few stray flakes of snow against his face. He had a dozen steps the start of the nearest pursuers, and in the night and confusion, that was plenty. Presently he reached his horse, with the others hopelessly mixed as to where he had gone.

Back at the Longhorn buildings, there was still plenty of activity, bobbing lanterns here and there and men running like hounds trying to pick up a lost scent. But there was no move to get horses. Trying to find him in the night was hopeless, and they knew it. Likewise, Wolf Masterson had strode across to the lighted doorway of the bunkhouse, and he was telling the crew, graphically and forcefully, exactly what he thought of killers who would stoop to murder. Stumpy grinned.

"Maybe this visit wasn't quite wasted, at that," he reflected. "It's sure made Wolf do some thinkin' on his own account."

But Wolf's own words to him had confirmed that he intended to ride with this crew in the morning, to cross on to the Saddle and take his herd or die in the attempt. Stumpy's face was grave. If the cantankerous old rannyhan had only kept his mouth shut and given him a chance to explain, Stumpy had held high hopes of reaching an understanding. Now it didn't look like there was any chance of that at all.

So far as a pitched battle was concerned, the prospect wouldn't have worried Stumpy particularly if it hadn't been for Wolf. He had a bigger crew than Cloud could muster, and though none of them was a professional gunman, they all knew how to use a six-shooter, and Stumpy preferred such a crew at his back, any day. He had rather expected such a battle to come, sooner or later—and it might as well be now.

Except for Wolf. How could he fight against the father of the girl he hoped one day to marry? It was a dark night, and he could see no light ahead.

Or could he? Stumpy straightened a little in the saddle, staring. The snow was still light, just a few scattering flakes, and he had topped a hill, from which it was possible to see a long way off to the south and east. And, showing like a pin-point at that distance, was unmistakably a light.

Stumpy studied it with narrowed eyes. It was miles away, which meant that it was a big fire to show at all at this distance. A bonfire, of course, down by the river—probably on the southern bank, where the nesters were still camped.

A fire such as that, which could be seen so far, must have some special significance. What was going on there, anyway? Far from anxious to return to the Saddle, where Gloria would probably be sitting up, waiting for him, and with such a report as he must bring, Stumpy turned his horse toward the beacon.

The fact that it continued to burn with undiminished brightness as time went on and the miles slipped under his horse's hoofs, was proof that it was some sort of a signal. Something must be in the offing, and this was a message to bring the homesteaders from miles around to conference.

It was snowing steadily now as he reached the river and crossed it. Now the big fire could be seen plainly, with people milling around it, ghostly figures in the red glare, and the deep curtain of blackness on all sides. There was a big crowd gathered there now, but others were still coming—men on horseback, wrapped against the storm, riding in singly or by twos and threes. As he had guessed, this big fire was a beacon, and the nesters were answering its call, demonstrating the hold that Bannack had gained over a whole countryside.

The big fire could be seen for a long way, of course, and where it could not be seen, others who had glimpsed it would carry the word. Here was gathering a crew bigger than Mart Cloud could muster, men who came, grim-faced, armed with rifles, shotguns or six-guns. Whatever the cause, most of the homesteaders were getting here now, and the real business of the meeting seemed about to begin.

Without dismounting, Stumpy rode closer, keeping back in the darkness, where he could see and hear, but a little apart from others. He could make out the hulking figure of Tom Bannack by the fire, and he recognized a few others, among them Hankins and Radley.

At a gathering like this, he could make himself known safely enough, Stumpy supposed. He had been a friend to some of these men. But he much preferred to remain out of sight. He'd be apt to learn more, that way, and he had declined to throw in his lot with them, to make common cause in the fight against Cloud. After all, he was what they were not—a cattleman.

His horse danced impatiently, but Stumpy checked it and leaned forward in the saddle, ears straining. The hubbub of voices subsided as Bannack held up his hand.

"A lot of you are wonderin' what this is all about," he said. "Why I've routed you out on a night like this. Well, there's a plenty good reason. And I'm sure pleased that you've all responded the way yuh have to the signal. We've got a lot, by stickin' together. And by stickin' together, we're going to keep on and get the rest of this country."

"It's a plumb hell of a night tuh get us out here tuh listen to a speech," somebody complained.

"Yeah, it sure is," Bannack agreed. "But I'm going to do more'n talk, Jim Green. You've got a good homestead right now, but there's a lot of folks here tuhnight that ain't got a foot of land—and won't get any till Cloud is cleared off the Longhorn. Which is what we're going to do—tomorrow!"

There was an electric current of excitement through the crowd at his words. Bannack went on.

"I got word, this evenin', that Cloud and Masterson aim tuh take their crew, in the mornin', and head across and tackle Garford, on the Saddle. Garford's got the Wagon Wheel cattle, and Masterson aims tuh take 'em away from him. Which is all right with us—it'll keep 'em all occupied tomorrow."

"Garford's helped us out," someone said doubtfully.

"Sure. And we'll be helpin' him out, too. While the Long-

horn crew is over on his place, we'll be on the Longhorn—
and when they get back there, providin' they do, they won't
find much to come back to, or a nice reception, either.
They—"

Impatient from standing, knowing that other horses were
not far off in the darkness, Stumpy's cayuse whinnied suddenly. Before he could check it or make a move, other horsemen, whose presence he hadn't guessed at, mounted guards
back on the outskirts of the gathering, moved up swiftly
on either side of him, and he caught the reflected firelight
on gun-barrels. Someone growled a harsh order.

"Stick 'em up, Mister. We'll have a look at yuh—and no
foolin', 'less yuh want to chaw on lead."

CHAPTER 16

THE SUDDENNESS of the move by which he had been surrounded was a surprise. Stumpy hadn't given the nesters
credit for taking such precautions, but this was just another
evidence that Tom Bannack was a leader who was worthy
of respectful attention.

Stumpy shrugged and submitted to having his horse led
out into the circle of firelight. The snowflakes, falling steadily, made a swishing curtain of white with crimson tints
against the black backdrop of the night, and men crowded
closer, staring, exclaimed in surprise as they recognized
him. Bannack strode forward.

"Who we got here?" he demanded, and when someone informed him excitedly, his face did not change.

"So you're Garford, eh?" he nodded. "You're the hombre
that told us the Wagon Wheel 'd put up a scrap."

They regarded each other with disfavor. It had become
clear to Stumpy some time before that Bannack was jealous
of him, because Stumpy, in his operations, had attracted a
lot of attention.

Bannack had know that Gloria was regarded as Stumpy's
girl, and, perhaps for that reason as much as any other, he
had tried to get her for himself, had boasted openly that
sooner or later she'd have to come to him.

His words as well as his looks were insulting now, and
deliberately so. It was Bannack's nature to be overbearing,
and with the cattlemen he had followed, from the first, a

studied policy of treating them as though they were the cattle they owned. And in his eyes now it was easy to see that he regarded Stumpy exactly as Stumpy regarded himself—as a cattleman.

"Didn't the Wagon Wheel fight hard enough to suit you?" Stumpy asked mildly.

Bannack snorted.

"Call that a scrap?" he demanded, and shrugged the Wagon Wheel aside as of no consequence. "How long yuh been settin' here, gettin' an earful?"

"Long enough to hear what you're plannin' to do to the Longhorn in the morning."

"What's the idea, settin' out there like a sneak?"

Stumpy leaned forward, but a man stepped swiftly forward from the background.

"That ain't no way to talk to him, Tom," he protested. "Mr. Garford is as good a friend as any of us homesteaders have ever had. He's as much right here as anybody else."

Bannack shrugged, but he let it go at that, and Stumpy did the same.

"Well, you clean 'em out at your end, and we'll tend to the nest they come from," Bannack went on. "Tell you what. You've got a big crew, and so have we. Mebby it's lucky you come along. We can work out somethin' to trap them unsuspectin', same as they've done to us, and mow them down before they have a chance."

"Shoot them from ambush, you mean?" Stumpy challenged.

"That's what they done to us, didn't they?"

"Reckon it is. But I'm no murderer, even if some others are."

Bannack's jowls reddened like the wattles of a turkey gobbler.

"You callin' me a murderer?" he demanded.

"You're namin' your own poison, hombre."

There was a moment's tense silence. But from the little murmur which went around the ring of homesteaders, it was apparent that they disapproved of all this. Bannack controlled himself with an effort, realizing that he had gone too far. These men, as a whole, were not of his stamp, and he knew it.

"Well, how about it?" he demanded. "We ain't got no

cause to quarrel, Garford. Not when our int'rests run the same. Are you throwin' in with us, or not?"

"Nothing doing," Stumpy retorted. "If the Longhorn, or anybody else, tries to come on my land, lookin' for trouble, they'll get all they want of it. But that's as far as I go."

It was not a diplomatic answer. But there had been plenty of blame on both sides. And since he was a cattleman himself, he wasn't going to throw in with the man who had evicted Gloria from her home, who now proposed cold-blooded murder. For one thing was abundantly clear. Whoever went along with Tom Bannack would follow him as leader. There could be no divided leadership here.

Bannack listened incredulously. His face reddened, and then the explosion came.

"So yuh won't play along with us, eh?" he growled. "Well, yuh boys heard him—and you all know what scripture says. He that ain't for us is against us."

"The devil can quote scripture as well as anybody else," Stumpy prodded. Usually he was cautious, but now his anger was rising to a point where he didn't care. Certainly he wasn't afraid of Bannack.

Bannack shook his head, as though patient under unjust persecution.

"You've heard him refuse to work with us, even when it sounded like our interests all run the same way," he went on. "And there always has tuh be a reason for such things, boys. Either a man's for you, or he's ag'in yuh. He's against us, and I'll tell you why. Because he's always been a cattle-man, and he still makes his brags that he's a cattleman."

"You're right for once," Stumpy agreed.

"Hear that? Well, I'll tell you boys something else. A cattleman ain't no homesteader—and he ain't no friend of us, callin' us nesters and squatters an' all the rest. Since we've got to have a showdown sooner or later, we'll just have it now, and keep Mr. Stumpy Garford right here. His cowboys ain't homesteaders—they're just tryin' tuh steal that land from real homesteaders, turnin' it over to him. But this is one time yuh made a mistake, Mr. Cattleman. We—"

Stumpy had been watching narrowly. Before his eyes, Bannack had demonstrated why he was a leader. A few minutes before, he had made a declaration which nearly all of them resented. Yet now, with a few words and a per-

sonality which indisputably swayed men as the wind bends
a sapling—and it was mostly the man, rather than his words
—he had brought them under his spell again, ready to do
whatever he suggested.

And Stumpy knew that he had only a handful of friends
in this gathering, and they would be helpless against the
crowd. Most of the nesters took Bannack's word that he was
a cattleman and therefore an enemy, and from a quality of
doubt as to his status a few minutes before, they had suddenly become dangerous.

Stumpy moved fast. His hand had been quietly toying
with the rope tied beside his saddle-horn, and now he shook
it out, sending the loop straight for the man in front of
him, without bothering with any preliminary swing. The
noose settled around Bannack's shoulders before he quite
realized what was happening, and the next instant, at a
touch of the spurs, Stumpy's horse whirled, was away like a
startled jackrabbit.

Stumpy held to the rope just long enough to start Bannack at a run, almost but not quite jerking him off his feet,
and completely spoiling whatever he had had in mind. Then,
letting go the rope, the cowboy was through them and swallowed in the dark and storm.

"And that wasn't so bad," he chuckled, as his cayuse
splashed out on to the far shore of the river. "Only it loses
me a good rope. And by rights, it ought to have been about
his neck and kept there."

For he was under no delusions as to what this meant.
Bannack had declared war, back there, in saying that
Stumpy's cowboys were no real homesteaders, and that there
had to be a showdown between them, sooner or later.

It came as no surprise to Stumpy. Knowing the sort of
man that Bannack was, he had foreseen that, once the other
available land in the country was taken up, Bannack would
turn inevitably to try and break up the last remaining big
ranch. The fact that the cowboys had legally filed on the
claims meant nothing to him. There were ways of jumping
claims, even on such a scale.

If Stumpy could be killed, most of his men would quickly
lose interest and either leave voluntarily or sell their rights
for a song. Spending three years to get hold of a piece of
land for the sake of the ground would never appeal to men

of their nature. Or if they could be driven off or killed—or even failing that, there were ways of contesting a claim.

So now Bannack would war with them as well. Stumpy's smile was grim. His interests were one with those of Mart Cloud, and yet Cloud was doing everything he could to destroy him.

The storm was thickening. The air was full of heavy, wet flakes which melted as they fell, but they were cold and raw for all of that. And it was a long way on to the home buildings, though he was already on his own land. Besides, it was dark as a pocket, the ground was muddy, slick underfoot.

Off at the side loomed something a little darker than the rest of the night, and Stumpy turned toward it. This was one of the homestead shacks which had been built on runners and hauled into position. This one was setting half on Stumpy's own quarter-section, half on the hundred and sixty belonging to Chinook. One or the other of them, sometimes both, usually spent the night there. Tonight it was Chinook's turn, but Stumpy turned toward it. He'd wait for daylight before going the rest of the way, a night like this.

There was a certain amount of danger for his cowboys, even in pairs, spread over the thousands of acres of the Saddle, sleeping out in these lonely shacks. Also, it was a lot more trouble for them to go and return again, than it would have been to bunk at the main headquarters.

But Stumpy intended to do the thing up in a legal manner. The law stipulated that men who filed on a homestead should live there a certain number of days out of each year, and that meant sleeping on it.

Hundreds of miles away, a few years before, Stumpy had witnessed another clash between homesteaders and big landholders. There, however, the landholders had recognized the encroaching danger of the nesters and had taken steps to protect themselves, in the same manner that he was doing here—by having their cowboys, or their herders, if they were sheepmen, file on the land and hold it for them.

Only their method was different. None of them had gone to the formality of building claim shacks or having their men sleep on the land at all, except by accident, if their work happened to take them across it. The only gesture toward living there or improving the land during the three years necessary to prove up, had been that the boss would run his cattle or sheep over it.

In that manner, and others of a similar nature, hundreds of thousands of acres had been acquired, with titles from the government, and no word of protest ever raised. In many cases, it was the best thing, for bona-fide homesteaders would only have starved trying to make a living off such land as was offered them. Sometimes, however, it had amounted to an outright steal of choice ground.

Stumpy was under no illusions as to what he was doing. He was fighting for himself and for those he loved, to try and preserve something which had been a lifetime in the building. And his methods were as honest as those used against him. Moreover, he insisted on living up to the letter of the law—that his men should actually live on their land as required by law, despite the inconvenience or the danger.

He found the shack empty, the stove cold. Chinook had not been there at all that night. Which was nothing unusual or anything to worry about. Stumpy shed his wet outer clothes, crawled between his blankets, and was instantly asleep. There would be plenty to worry about on the morrow, but that was time enough to worry.

The slam of a bullet, tearing through the boards above his head, awakened him jerkily. He sat bolt upright, and was instantly aware of somebody beside him, likewise sitting up in the darkness. Chinook's voice came, cool and undisturbed, but faintly annoyed.

"And just as I was gettin' intuh the middle of a right pleasant dream! Durn, looks like we got callers, Stumpy."

So Chinook had finally arrived, rather late, had crawled in beside him without disturbing Stumpy. The realization that he was there, with an attack coming, was comforting.

Outside, there sounded a sudden chorus of yells, more bullets splintered through the boards above their heads, the slam of guns was thunderous in the heavy blackness.

"Seems as though we have," Stumpy agreed. "And sendin' in their cards in advance. Well, you take that end, Chinook, and I'll hold this one. Nothin' like givin' them a warm welcome."

CHAPTER 17

THE SHOOTING had stopped, now. It was getting toward morning, and apparently the storm had ceased as well, for it was getting light enough in the shack to see dimly. All at once there was a new sound—the crackling of flames, a faint curl of smoke from the far end of the building. Despite the snow, it was dry enough underneath, and they had sneaked up under cover of the gunfire to build a fire there.

Now a voice sounded, harsh and peremptory.

"We've got yuh dead to rights, hombre! And yuh'd ought to know by now that the Longhorn don't bluff! Come out uh there, Chinook, with yore hands up—or yuh won't come a-tall!"

Chinook, backing away from where the fire was starting to eat through, glanced at Stumpy questioningly. Stumpy nodded.

"Go ahead, like they say, Chinook," he whispered. "I'll give 'em a little surprise party."

They didn't know, then, that he was here. They figured instead that Chinook was all alone, and that they had him dead to rights. And in that, had he been alone, there was little doubt that they were right. With fire to drive him out if he tried to make a fight of it, and the shack surrounded, his position would have been hopeless.

Stumpy was doubly sure now of who the attackers were. That reference to the Longhorn had removed his last doubt. They were Bannack's men, for the Longhorn wouldn't have betrayed themselves.

"Better be comin' pronto, Chinook!" the voice yelled again.

"I'm comin'," Chinook agreed, and pushed open the door, his hands in the air. He stepped outside, into the murky dawn light, and advanced a few steps. The others quickly converged around him—five of them, homesteaders unmistakably, though they were dressed in cowboy garb.

"So yuh're the foreman of this spread, eh?" one of them jeered. "And that's what I call a plumb crime, eh, boys?"

"A hangin' crime, if yuh ask me," was the retort.

"A hangin' crime is right. Get that rope, somebody, and we'll put it to a good use—and teach folks that it don't pay to buck the Longhorn."

The whole thing was too pat, too cut and dried. One man was bringing a rope, which Stumpy recognized as his own, that he had left around Bannack's shoulders earlier in the night. They intended to leave the shack a pile of ashes, and

Chinook hanging from a tree, to make it look like Longhorn work. Which would doubly infuriate the Saddle, as they figured it, and ensure a clash to the death between the two outfits which they aimed to destroy.

It had gone far enough. Besides, the fire needed to be doused before it did serious damage. Stumpy's voice, drawling, came from the doorway, jerking them to startled attention.

"Lift 'em, boys—lift 'em high! That's right. No claim-jumpin' today—not around here. And you can tell Bannack that. Get their hardware, Chinook."

They stared, disgruntled at being recognized, while Chinook obeyed with alacrity. Stumpy motioned with his gun.

"There's a couple buckets here—and the rest of you can use your hats. There's a spring right over there. Get that fire out, pronto!"

Under the baleful muzzles of his gun and Chinook's, they obeyed, dousing the blaze in a hurry. Stumpy inspected it, then waved his gun toward where their horses were grouped, off on the horizon.

"You can get going, now—and take a tip from me. The Saddle ain't a healthy climate to live on—not for hombres of your stripe. Don't stop this side of the river."

He watched them mount and ride away, then they went inside the cabin again. Chinook shook his head, grumbling.

"Dog-gone disgustin'," he growled. "They run like scared coyotes, soon as they get a chance. But what the blazes was nesters doing here, tryin' tuh play at being cowboys?"

Stumpy sat down, tugging at his stiff boots, and explained what had happened south of the river during the night. Chinook whistled.

"One thing, times sure ain't dull here, north of the river," he commented. "You have any luck with the old Wolf, last evenin'?"

"I was lucky to get out of there with a whole hide, if that's what you mean," Stumpy confessed, and recounted that episode as well. He stood up and kicked the door shut.

"Likely the Longhorn will be coming for a call, today, same as they planned on," he went on. "And when they do, Bannack will try to sneak in and burn them out, there's no doubt of that. He was mad before, and he'll be plumb disgruntled now. Think you could manage to warn the Longhorn, as they come, without gettin' yourself a hide full of lead?"

"Ought to be able to," Chinook agreed. He had stuffed dry wood into the combination heater and cookstove, and was slicing bacon into a skillet, working by the light of a lantern. "If I see 'em—and I'll be right careful tuh see 'em first—I'll wave me a white rag or somethin', 'fore they start shootin'."

Stumpy nodded, dropping a handful of coffee into the pot and sliding it on to the stove. He was giving Chinook a risky job, but the Longhorn crew had to be warned if possible, and for a double reason. Though they might be at war now, their long-range interests were identical, and today it was up to him to help the Longhorn if possible. Likewise, anything which would help to improve relations right now was highly desirable.

In addition, there was a good chance of averting the Longhorn's attack on the Saddle, if they could be warned and sent back to guard their own place. If such an attack could be staved off, their own difficulties could be ironed out by a conference.

So it had to be done, doubly so because Wolf Masterson would be riding with the Longhorn. But it was a dangerous job to carry that message. Stumpy would have done it himself, but he knew, as Chinook also recognized, that Chinook would stand a far better chance of succeeding.

"I'll ride on home and be ready—just in case," Stumpy added, pouring the coffee as Chinook dished fried spuds and bacon on to a couple of tin plates.

"Nothin' like bein' ready," Chinook agreed, and took a gulp of coffee, then looked mildly startled.

"Me, I like cawfee," he sighed. "Fact is, I'm willin' to drink a lot of water, sometimes, tuh get a little of it. But ain't you kind of overdone it the other way, Stumpy? That's strong enough tuh get right up on its hind laigs and walk off —and mebby carry this shack with it, if necessary."

"Guess it is a mite above the weak point," Stumpy conceded. "Well, I'll be seein' you, Chinook."

He reached home in time for another breakfast with the rest of the crew, reporting what had transpired during the night. Gloria listened with big eyes, her face troubled.

"It could be a lot worse," Stumpy reassured her. "I didn't

get to talk things over with your dad, but he showed me what I'd known all along—that he wasn't a killer, and didn't side in with Cloud at all on this ambush stuff. I'm hopin' that we'll get things ironed out today. Chinook's pretty good, that way. And after this, they'd ought to see reason."

"I hope so," Gloria agreed fervently. "Oh, Stumpy, if anything was to happen to you—I—I just couldn't stand it."

"I'll take mighty good care that nothing happens," he agreed, and forced a grin, then turned as a messenger came on the run.

"The Longhorn's crossed our line," he reported briefly. "They're comin' in a bunch, and full force."

Stumpy's grin was wiped away. That looked ominous. What had happened to Chinook? He should have reached them long since, if at all. And then, as they turned, it was to see a rideless horse trotting up to the buildings, head held to one side so that the dragging reins did not impede it.

Cold seemed to reach Stumpy's heart. There was but one horse on the Saddle which would do that trick, rather than stand hitched by the dropped reins. Chinook's horse. He crossed swiftly to it, his jaw tightening.

There were blood-stains, scarcely dry, on the empty saddle.

CHAPTER 18

SOMETHING had gone wrong, and trouble was riding to the thundering hoofbeats of the Longhorn. Snow covered the ground now in a patchy blanket, torn and scuffed here and there where the querulous wind had kicked at it. Overhead now, the sun was tearing at the clouds which had laid the blanket, tumbling them wildly and making occasional holes where the sun shone briefly through and was gone again. It was a blustery, raw day, with skies that would soon be spitting leaden hail, from all the signs.

Stumpy's jaw tightened as he gazed at the empty, blood-stained saddle. That had all the look of murder. Of an ambush bullet, treacherously triggered and feathered with the venom of vengeance. Vengeance directed not primarily at Chinook, but aimed to strike through him at Stumpy.

It was that thought which caused him to hesitate. Right now, the Saddle and the Longhorn were two lone outfits left

against the world, and their every interest lay in working
together. To clash now would be suicidal. But Mart Cloud
was coming, looking for trouble—

Stumpy made his decision swiftly. Wolf Masterson was
Gloria's father. And the interests of the two cattle outfits
did lie together, whatever Cloud might think. Whatever
he did today was a gamble, but one course was suicidal, the
other might work. Stumpy swung into the saddle as someone ran up with his horse. Most of the crew were already
mounted, waiting, sitting sternly erect or looking to guns
in a last-minute inspection. Gloria looked up at him, her face
drained of color.

"You—you'll be careful, Stumpy?" she pleaded. "Doubly
so—today?"

Stumpy nodded.

"We won't clash with the Longhorn—not this morning,"
he promised, and saw the sudden light flow back into her
eyes. He waved briefly to his crew, swung away at a gallop.
But instead of heading to the northwest, where the Longhorn was crossing the line, they would swing off toward the
southwest.

He saw the puzzlement on the faces of his men as they
followed, but they asked no questions, though this course was
leading them away from the invaders. Stumpy knew that he
was gambling, this time, and if he made the wrong guess
it could be serious. But two and two together usually added
up to four.

They rode for a while, sheltered now by timber and the
long slope of the hills. Down in here there was peace, no
sight or sound of anything from the outside world. Even the
snow, protected from the wind, was unbroken, except for
the criss-crossing tracks of rabbits, with here and there the
jumpy trail of a predatory weasel or the long, loping gallop
of a coyote.

Then they topped the slope and pulled to a stop. There was
a long view from here, and Stumpy had counted on that
from the start. Ahead and below was the Dry Fork, the
main dividing line between the Saddle and the Longhorn,
scarcely more than a trickle of water in it now.

Off to the north, pigmy-like with distance, they could see
the Longhorn crew, still coming on, penetrating deeper into
Saddle territory, but moving more slowly now, wary of a

trap. Stumpy gave hardly a second glance to them.

For, still farther away, but riding fast, off to the west and south, was another band of mounted men, moving faster but in more ragged formation—nesters, mounted on plow horses and sorry nags of all descriptions, heading in on the unprotected Longhorn. Bannack was making good his threat to strike when the Longhorn was unprepared.

"There's our meat," said Stumpy, and led the way.

Understanding had come to his crew now. Which was more than could be said for the Longhorn. Riding out in sight as the Saddle had done, it was natural that the invaders should see them, and notice that the men of the Saddle were heading for the now unprotected Longhorn. That was what Stumpy had counted on.

It was a three-cornered race now, one in which only Stumpy and his men fully understood what was happening. For the far-off nesters had seen them coming, and were redoubling their efforts to reach the Longhorn buildings ahead of them and sow destruction as they went.

But the nesters had not seen the Longhorn crew, who, not seeing the nesters, and believing that Stumpy's men were intent on striking at their unprotected buildings, had turned and were heading straight back in an effort to get there ahead of them.

All three forces were riding desperately now, all with a common goal and widely varying plans, and still the sweep of the hills kept the two main opposing forces from sighting each other. But from where he rode, able to catch an occasional glimpse of both groups, Stumpy's face relaxed a little.

"It ought to be close, between the two of them," he said.

Red, riding close beside him, nodded.

"Reckon they're both in for a big surprise," he agreed.

Things seemed to be working out better than Stumpy had dared hope for, a little while before. It looked as if the Longhorn would beat the nesters, and as the two outfits raced, Stumpy slowed. The Saddle men who rode with him were hidden from sight of both rival outfits now.

As they topped a timbered slope, Stumpy pulled his badly blown horse to a stop, sitting there inside the curtain of trees. That wasn't his quarrel off there—it was between Mart Cloud and Tom Bannack, and since he had averted a clash between himself and Masterson, Stumpy didn't greatly care how this other scrap went. But Mart Cloud must understand now that Stumpy had acted as a friend in luring him back to the defense of his own ranch.

Stumpy watched with strained attention. Distances, in a country like this, were deceiving, more particularly where natural obstacles could turn riders aside or slow them down. It had looked, a few minutes before, as if the Longhorn would win the race. By now, both groups of riders had seen each other and now they both understood what was in the wind, but that had not caused either one to turn or slow down.

The nesters were redoubling their effort to get to the buildings first, the cattlemen were trying as desperately to save them. But now a stretch of swampy ground had slowed Cloud's men, and Bannack's were gaining. From the hilltop, miles away, Stumpy and his crew watched the unfolding of the drama.

By now, mounted on faster horses than the rest, several of the nesters had reached the buildings. Still a good half-mile away, Cloud and his crew sent a hail of lead at them, and under that blasting, one man lurched wildly in the saddle, swayed like a falling tree and collapsed. But the others had jumped from their horses and gained the shelter of the buildings.

It was as grim a race then as any of the watchers had ever witnessed, but the odds were with the nesters. Stumpy could see the ponderous figure of Bannack himself, who had been among the first to arrive, standing there in the shelter of one of the sheds and directing operations.

This was arson, open and brutal. The barn leaped to a blazing column of flame first, showing that there had been hay in it. Other buildings, including the house, were beginning to belch smoke edged with crimson before the desperate owners could reach the scene. And by that time the men who had started the fires had regained their horses and ridden to join their main force, just now coming up.

Some of the nesters had swung aside for another job, doing it swiftly. Not more than a mile from the buildings, the bulk of the beef herd of the Longhorn had been grazing, bunched compactly, proof enough that they had been recently gathered by a lot of hard riding.

Whatever Cloud's purpose in the round-up **might** have

been, the cattle were being scattered again now, stampeded by a waving of blankets and wild popping of guns. The ruthless thoroughness of Bannack was apparent now in every move. And the nesters, remembering the flooded river and the attack from ambush on this same land, were doing their job with a grimness equal to that of Tom Bannack himself.

The battle was joining now. The nesters could still have escaped by running, after spreading destruction, but Bannack was too crafty a leader to try anything like that. He wanted to stay and hold the Longhorn in play until the buildings were so well aflame that there could be no possibility of saving them. Likewise, he was anxious to strike a telling blow at Cloud, now that the opportunity offered.

Also, it was at least as safe to fight back, as to run and have the angry Longhorn on their flanks, like a swarm of hornets.

Guns were flaming, horses plunging wildly, the mounting columns of smoke from the now doomed buildings adding to the confusion. There was no fire-fighting equipment here, and no chance to use it if there had been. Already the flames had spread to engulf the smaller, outlying structures. The heart of the Longhorn was doomed.

It was still anybody's battle, with the opposing forces fairly equal in numbers and all of them wrought up to a fighting pitch. Stumpy watched bleakly. This was the sort of thing that he had foreseen and tried to prevent. If Wolf Masterson and Cloud's crew had been willing to let him talk, the night before, there might be a different story now.

"Looks like some more nesters comin'," Red commented, and pointed.

Stumpy followed the sweep of his arm, and shook his head. His quick glance had caught the gleam of the fugitive winter sunlight on badges. Nearly a dozen men rode in the new party—but these men were neither nesters nor cattlemen.

"That's the law," Stumpy said. "Looks like Vaughan—but there's a Federal Marshal headin' 'em up, I'll give you odds."

CHAPTER 19

THERE COULD be little question as to why the law was riding this way, onto the Longhorn. They had come to enforce Uncle Sam's edict and to protect the homesteaders in the rights which the government had granted to them, and the Longhorn was the seat of the trouble.

But they had arrived ahead of schedule, so far as Bannack was concerned. He hadn't planned to be caught in the act of trespass, red-handed with murder and arson, by those whom he had sent for to destroy the other side. Now, if either Wolf Masterson or Cloud had the sense to see and appreciate this new factor, they had it in their power to turn the tables neatly on Bannack and his crew.

Once more, there was nothing that Stumpy could do but watch. They were too far away to intervene, and it was too risky and unprofitable a business to get mixed in, in any case. The question now was, who would have the brains to profit by the coming of the law?

It was easy to see that the posse was as surprised as any of the others. About the last thing which they had expected was to ride in to the middle of a pitched gun-battle, with flaming buildings for a backdrop. But the men who rode in the lead were not the kind to temporize or hesitate in the face of danger. One of them was Sheriff Cliff Vaughan, who, with a federal man to take the lead, had crossed Saddle River at last. The other leader of the posse was plainly a marshal, and they were heading straight for where the fight was hottest.

Stumpy could guess their intention. As lawmen, it was, first of all, their duty to keep the peace. Right now they aimed, if it was humanly possible, to stop this fight, then to find out what it was all about and take appropriate action.

And it was apparent that the nesters, Bannack included, were dismayed as they recognized the posse and what their coming might mean.

It was then, while things hung by a hair, that the headlong rage of Cloud and Masterson swung the scales. They too had been dismayed by sight of the law. Wolf Masterson was remembering that he was an outlaw, and that these men had come for him; and Cloud, in a moment of unreasoning panic,

98

knew that he was wanted as a killer who had defied this same law, a man who had given shelter to an outlaw. Neither of them stopped to think beyond that.

It was Cloud who fired the first shot on the lawmen, but some of the others were close behind him.

"The fools!" Stumpy gritted his teeth. "The blind, crazy fools!"

That had done it. By holding off, pointing to their own burning buildings and the crew they were fighting against, Cloud could have charged the nesters with attack and arson, and have shown the proof. Automatically bettering his own condition and putting the others in bad.

But by firing on the lawmen, he had forced them automatically to fight with the nesters, and Tom Bannack was swift to take advantage of the break. Below them now, Stumpy and his men could see the enactment of a brutal drama. Men were fighting, off there, and dying, but with the coming of the lawmen, the odds had shifted heavily and decisively in favor of the nesters.

For a little while the Longhorn resisted fiercely, stubbornly. Then a bullet lifted Mart Cloud out of the saddle, so that he toppled, hung caught by one foot in a stirrup while his horse reared, whirled, and plunged away in terror, that pitiful thing which had been a man bumping and dragging behind until finally the foot jerked loose and the horse ran unimpeded.

The death of Cloud broke the fighting spirit of his crew. Wolf Masterson, a leader of no mean caliber, was in what looked like half a dozen places at once, trying to rally them, but it was too late, and hopeless in any case. Several of them threw down their guns and quit. Others broke and ran, and a handful of them managed to get away, Wolf Masterson among them. The battle was over as abruptly as it had begun, and from the hilltop, it appeared to be a complete victory for the nesters. The Longhorn had been wiped out, as swiftly and decisively as had happened with the Wagon Wheel.

A little sick at what he had witnessed, Stumpy turned his horse and led the way back to the Saddle. There was nothing that he could do off there—there had been nothing at any time, beyond what he had tried to accomplish.

If Cloud had only had a little farsightedness, or clear

judgment when it was required, he had been given three perfect chances in the last twenty-four hours to win. Stumpy had given him two of them, the arrival of the lawmen had afforded the third. He had muffed every chance, and had paid the price of failure.

There would be no further threat from the Longhorn, but its fall left the Saddle to stand alone, and Stumpy was under no illusions. Bannack was flushed with triumph, and Bannack hated him. The battle from now on would be more bitter than ever. And Wolf Masterson was now, past any changing, an outlaw, a hunted man with a price on his head. He had joined in the fight against lawmen, local and federal.

A horse snorted, and as they swung to see the cause, the rider was out of the saddle and kneeling beside something there in the snow and tall grass. Stumpy pushed closer, swung down.

The snow was stained and trampled, and Chinook lay there, his face as white as the snow except for a stain of dried blood down the right temple and cheek. But he was alive, and examination brought hope. A rifle bullet had knocked him out of the saddle, creasing the side of his head, a nasty wound which had bled a lot, but it hadn't been quite deep enough to kill him.

"And that," Stumpy said between his teeth, "is another score to settle with Tom Bannack and his nesters!"

The others nodded, grim-faced. There could be little doubt but what it had been a Bannack-inspired bullet which had stopped Chinook. The Longhorn had been riding, miles away, when it had happened, and that put them out of the reckoning. Bannack or some of his men had seen Chinook heading for the Longhorn, had guessed at the message he carried, one which, delivered, would have saved the Longhorn and averted the threat of a clash between the two cattle outfits. So Chinook had been shot as callously as Cloud in turn had fired on homeseekers.

"Seems tuh me there's somethin' in Scriptur' about the feller that takes a sword, perishin' by the bullet," Red commented unexpectedly, while his companions stared in amazement that he should quote scripture. "Well, seems to have worked out that way for Cloud."

Going slowly now, carrying Chinook, they had barely reached the home buildings when new riders came into sight, jogging toward them unhurriedly. Cliff Vaughan was in the lead. With him were several of his posse, though Stumpy did not see the man with a marshal's badge. There were a couple of homesteaders, men strangers to Stumpy, but whom he had seen in the circle of firelight by the river, the night before.

They rode up amid a sudden tense silence, and Cliff Vaughan dismounted, though the others remained mounted, watchful and alert. The sheriff nodded.

"Mornin', Stumpy. So this is your place, eh?"

"Morning, Sheriff," Stumpy returned. "Yeah, this is my place."

"Nice layout you've got here. Getting ready for winter, looks like."

"We're trying to. And it looks like you've changed your mind—about not havin' jurisdiction north of the river."

Vaughan nodded, removing his hat to stare at it thoughtfully, then replacing it.

"Yes. There's two reasons for that—maybe three. One being that you came north of the river, and things have changed a lot since then. Then the people down there, the commissioners and so on, workin' with the state, they decided that I didn't have enough trouble as it was, and voted me jurisdiction up here. One of those things you get without wantin' them. Then, last night, McGill, the U. S. Marshal, blew in, and when he headed this way and asked me to come along—well, I guess that explains it."

"That explains it, all right," Stumpy agreed watchfully. He knew Cliff Vaughan of old. When he was so very precise and careful, that was the time to look out. He believed in doing things in orderly fashion, but when he started a job, he had a habit of seeing it through.

"Reckon you saw what happened, over on the Longhorn?" Vaughan asked abruptly. "We saw some of you toppin' that hill, on your way back."

"We had a pretty good view," Stumpy conceded. "Looked like a bad mess."

"Plenty bad," the sheriff agreed soberly. "McGill is still over there, kind of lookin' after things. With Cloud killed, it changes the picture. Leaves the land all open to settlement now, of course, and McGill aims to keep order. Besides which, he took a bullet through his arm. So I came over here to ask a few questions."

"I'm listenin'."

"Yeah. Well, I've explained about my jurisdiction, Stumpy. So—what about your burnin' the buildings of the Longhorn, bringin' the homesteaders and the Longhorn together in a bloody scrap, then sneakin' out of it?"

CHAPTER 20

STUMPY STARED, startled for a moment. Then he understood, and gave grudging admiration to the nimble mind and adroit sidestepping of Tom Bannack.

"So that's how Bannack tried to explain it, eh?" Stumpy asked thoughtfully.

The sheriff nodded.

"That's how he explains it. Now I'm askin' how you do."

"I'm glad you've got an open mind, Cliff. Not that we need it, for we've plenty of proof for my story. We found out that Longhorn was coming over this way today, which they started to do, to take the Wagon Wheel cattle over to the Longhorn range. They came in force, expecting us to put up a fight. And I found out that Bannack knew of their plans, and aimed to burn the Longhorn out while they were away."

Vaughan was watching him, his face expressionless. He nodded.

"Go on."

"So, when Longhorn did come, we all started for there, to try and save their buildings for them—preferrin' that to a scrap, when we'd do better to work together. Time we got to that hill, we saw we were too late. But by that time, seein' us ridin' that way and mistakin' the fact that we were going to pay a friendly call, Cloud had turned and was getting home again. Bannack's men were ahead of us, and so were Cloud's, so we didn't go ny farther. Bannack and a few of his men got there ahead of the Longhorn. That's the story."

He did not amplify it. If Vaughan wanted proof, there was plenty of it to be found. The unbroken snow, beyond the hill where they had watched the battle, would convince any man who knew the country, that they had gone no farther. And there was the testimony of his entire crew.

The sheriff nodded, satisfied.

"That seems to put you in the clear, all right," he agreed,

and smiled a little wryly. "Looks like a hard winter," he added, and swung back into the saddle, jingled away with his posse behind him.

Stumpy understood. So far as he was concerned, things were all right. Bannack had been just a little too adroit in explaining things away that time, and had been caught in a lie. Not that it would make any difference to Bannack or his men now.

Had Cloud taken advantage of the breaks, he could have saved his ranch and seen Bannack and the handful of ring-leaders who approved of such methods, lodged safely behind prison walls for a long time. That would have been enough, coupled with the murderous attack on the ranch, to have cleared Cloud's record again and given him a fresh chance to save his land by the method which Stumpy was using.

But Cloud had missed his chance, and by the same token, Bannack and his homesteaders were in the clear now, since they had fought on the side of the law before the battle was finished. The fact that outlaws had lost their buildings would be charged off, particularly since Cloud was dead and his outfit would be parceled out among the homeseekers before the day was over.

It left Bannack the winner, his hold stronger than ever on the nesters. And it left Wolf Masterson a man with a price on his head, ranging the far hills with a small band of other hunted men who had elected to stick with him.

Back on the Saddle, Chinook was making a gradual improvement. He grinned up at Stumpy and cocked his head to the howl of a snowstorm raging outside.

"All that's wrong with me, aside from general cussed-ness, is that I've got a lazy streak," he confessed. "It's a lot nicer to stay in yore bunk, weather like this, than tuh go chasin' around out in the cold. Come spring, yuh'll see me just as lively as ever."

It was only a few days, in reality, until Chinook was pretty much his usual self again, but by that time winter had really closed down on the country, fastening an icy hand which kept activity at a minimum. On the Saddle, the buildings were ready for the winter, however, the big herd was in good shape, and so far as weather was concerned, Stumpy had no cause for worry.

Across the line the situation was a grimmer one. One man

had really profited from the dissolution of the Longhorn, and that man was Tom Bannack. Just how he had managed it, few men bothered to inquire too closely, but in the space of a few short weeks Bannack had risen to both wealth and power. He had gotten hold of Mart Cloud's big herd of cattle, and while the herd had vanished from the newly home-steaded range, the profits had flowed back to Bannack's pockets.

Bannack had started a new store, north of the river. More than that, he had built a new town. Almost overnight it blossomed, first with the general store, followed in swift succession by a saloon and secondary mercantile establish-ments. Prices were high, which was only to be expected, since everything had to be freighted in from Fortymile. But if prices were high, credit was more than liberal.

To nesters who had rejoiced one day in victory over the Longhorn, and in a good piece of land, it had been a dis-couraging morning after, with winter closing down and no place to live. But Bannack had been more than helpful with lumber and supplies. Plenty of credit, and a saloon next door at which to get a drink to drive the chill from their bones before starting back home.

Stumpy was one of the first to see what was happening. Under the double stimulus of need and whiskey, these men were signing mortgages which they could never hope to repay.

"He's aimin' to do the same thing as me—only different," Stumpy said grimly. "Time these poor devils come to prove up, after puttin' in three years of work getting their land in a half-way decent shape, they'll find that Bannack owns the whole country. The main difference is that I'm hiring cow-boys and payin' them wages, and they know just what they're doing. These other fellows aim to have land of their own, but they're workin' just for a living—not even for wages."

Fortymile had become, all at once, a staid, almost respect-able town. But all of its old wildness had been transferred, untamed, to the new Bannack. Set amid a sprawling wilder-ness, untrammeled by even the shadow of law, it was Ban-nack's town, and anything went. Stumpy watched from a distance, and at his orders, no man from the Saddle patron-ized the new town.

"You go in there for a drink, and you'll be lucky to get out with a whole skin," Chinook adjured the cowboys. "And besides, it's not a cowman's town."

Because of Bannack's need for consolidating the vast holdings which had been taken over, and with the hampering weather as well, the Saddle was left pretty much alone for a time. But Stumpy was not fooled. Bannack had already made his threats, and now he was starting to make his boasts as well. With the coming of spring, and weather in which men could work, they would clean out this last cattle stronghold, and take over the Saddle as well.

All that was still on the outskirts, like a wolf pack lurking beyond the radius of a campfire. Of more immediate concern was the plight of Wolf Masterson. Somewhere, deep in the fastnesses of the hills, he had holed up with his followers, lonely, embittered, a man with a price on his head. Rumor said that other hunted men were joining him. And in this news there was little comfort for Gloria or Stumpy.

The latter had made several attempts to get in touch with Masterson and try and bring about a change for the better, not only in their own relations, but in Masterson's brush with the law. Once he had made a three-day trip back into the hills himself, but it had been like all the other tries. Wolf Masterson trusted no man, and he was a crafty old rannyhan. No one, lawmen or those who might represent the law, ever succeeded in finding him.

"I guess it's no use, till he gets ready to show up himself," Stumpy confessed to Gloria. "But so long as he keeps out of sight, the law isn't trying very hard to find him. That's something."

Gloria had been staring unseeingly out of the window, not noticing the undulating slopes of snow or the bitter wind whistling around the corners of the house. Now she turned to Stumpy, her lips trembling a little.

"It was awfully good of you to try, Stumpy," she said. "You've been so good in so many ways—and I've not been able to pay you at all for your kindness."

"Me?" Stumpy looked surprised. "I haven't done anything."

"You've done a lot. And I know what you want—even if you have been patient. And I'd like to marry you, Stumpy— nothing could make me happier. Only—only you'll have to be

patient a little longer. I—I couldn't marry you—not with my
father out there, ranging the hills like a hunted wolf, and
with a price on his head."

"That one angle of it wouldn't make a bit of difference
to me," Stumpy assured her.

"I know. But it would to me, Stumpy. I can't let you marry
an outlaw's daughter. Though it's cruel, to keep you out of
your own house, living in the bunkhouse—"

"Shucks. I've done that all my life—"

"And you shouldn't have to do it now. But that's the way
it is, Stumpy. While he's out there, that way, I—I just
can't."

Stumpy understood, and did not argue, but it was a dis-
couraging proposition. Wolf Masterson had become a rider
of the hoot-owl trails, and where the end of the trail might
be was more than Stumpy could see. If he did come back, the
law would inevitably send him to prison for a long term.
There seemed to be no turning on that stormy road.

A change was coming over Tom Bannack as the winter
wore on, or perhaps it was only the real Bannack showing
himself more plainly as he grew more powerful, more sure
of himself. For a while he had professed to be like any of the
others—just a homeseeker who had the same interests as
any of them. His victories had solidified his leadership, but
now men were coming to distrust him, some to actively hate
him. He was swaggering, arrogant, and he made no pretense
of living on his own homestead. There was more money to
be made in his new town, and where money could be made
was where he stayed.

For all that, he kept his hold on the countryside, by devious ways. Partly by a promise of more land for those who
wanted it, partly by fear, and in part by the hold he had ob-
tained on so many already. The profits of the Longhorn had
bought the bodies of men in turn, and some of them were
beginning to suspect the truth of that purchase.

It was a long winter, but the cattle on the Saddle wintered
well. That was cause for real satisfaction, for Stumpy had
been rushed in getting ready. But he had a big crew, and the
thing which counted most was that they were all loyal. And
they knew how to handle cattle.

The coming of spring saw a country changed out of all
recognition from what it had been a year before. The Sad-

dle was the last big cattle ranch where, one year earlier, cattle ranches had been the rule. Everywhere else were the small nesters.

The winter had witnessed a gradual change in their sentiment, one which Stumpy had realized was inevitable. The fact that he had befriended some of the homesteaders had helped him at first, and the added fact that he too was a somesteader had made him one of them, in their eyes.

But Bannack had been working steadily to change all that. There had been sickness at the Hankins home, and at his suggestion the children had been sent away to a doctor. Their mother had gone with them. Not long after, Hankins had needed money, and Bannack had paid cash, and generously, for the rights to Hankins' homestead, and had hold those rights to a newcomer at a loss. But he was not a man to begrudge a few dollars where it would pay big in the long run.

As spring began to make its appearance across the countryside, Bannack struck. Stumpy stepped to the door one morning in response to a knock, to find Bannack there, with a dozen other nesters behind him. They had ridden up so quietly as to attract no attention.

"Well?" Stumpy demanded.

"Pretty well," Bannack nodded jovially. He held out a sheaf of legal-looking papers. "Reckon you'll have to be gettin' off this land, Garford. We're contestin' every claim you have, and filin' on it legal."

CHAPTER 21

STUMPY EYED him narrowly. He had known for a long time that Bannack planned to start something, but he hadn't been quite certain as to what sort of a move he would make. Now it had come, and it was a move crefully calculated to cause Stumpy a lot of trouble. Stumpy wasn't making the mistake of underestimating Bannack. He was as clever as he was unscrupulous.

But if it came to bluff, Stumpy was as skilled at the art as Bannack could ever hope to be. He declined to accept the papers, shoving them back contemptuously.

"This is my land, Bannack," he said. "And you're trespassin'."

"Not interested, eh?" Bannack sneered. "Well, you'd better be. A lot of other fellows was sayin' the same thing, a few months back—men like Proctor and Cloud and Masterson. But they made a little mistake."

"Yeah. They never owned the land in the first place," Stumpy conceded. "But it's different, here on the Saddle. And I'm warning you. Anybody that tries to jump these claims, till the government gives him a clear go-ahead, is going to get more trouble than he can digest. Chew on that, Bannack."

"We'll have a go-ahead, right soon," Bannack said confidently. "We've charged that none of your filings were made in good faith, that every man on the Saddle is in your employ, and that they aim to turn the land over to you, not make homes of them. There'll be officers along in a day or so, to investigate—and when we prove the charges, you'll be out in the cold."

"When you prove them, I'll get off," Stumpy agreed. "Till you do, you get off—and stay. Start to movin' now!"

Bannack hesitated. His arrogance had increased with his power, and now it was easy to see that he was more than half drunk as well. Off by the house, Gloria had come to the door, surprised at the sight of visitors. Bannack waved jauntily.

"H'llo, sweetheart," he called. "I'm takin' this place over, but I'll let you keep that house for the two of us. I—"

He got no further. Stumpy hit him, a solid right to the chin which spun him around and back, staggering. It wasn't often that Stumpy went berserk, but this time he was seeing red.

Bannack, startled, ripped out an oath and charged back, swinging wildly. Stumpy came up under those flailing arms with solid jolts to the stomach which sent Bannack sprawling. Bannack's men, carefully picked, started to move forward, their faces ugly, but by now some of the Saddle crew were appearing. They moved forward, smiling grimly, hands on hips, and Chinook voiced a soft warning.

"That scrap there looks like sort of a private affair. But if so be as yuh hombres hone tuh make it public—"

He waited, and at the eagerness in his face and that of the others, who now outnumbered the nesters two to one, they backed away with swift disclaimers.

"Sure, it's a private affair," one of them agreed. "All we want is tuh see fair play."

"I'm right shocked tuh find myself in agreement with any of yore kind of critter," Chinook sighed. "But seems like yuh took the words right out of my mouth. Fair play is what we're aimin' tuh see—that, and tuh watch the boss give a good lickin' to yore polecat leader."

Stumpy grinned. He had a real fight on his hands, as he had known would be the case. Bannack was big, powerful, and he knew how to fight. But he had been living too soft during the winter, drinking too much liquor, and already it was beginning to tell on him. The knowledge that he couldn't last long made him desperate.

He came in fast, changed his tactics suddenly and lowered his head to butt. But Stumpy knew him too well to be caught napping. Bannack's hat had fallen off, his long hair was in wild disorder. Stumpy side-stepped, grabbed a handful of hair, and gave a twisting jerk which brought a bellow of pain from Bannack and sent him sprawling on the ground, sliding on his face for half a dozen feet.

Bannack raised up slowly, his face a bloody smear. Stumpy had stopped and was watching him, not moving. Only when Bannack had regained his feet did Stumpy see that he had found and clutched a good-sized rock in his fist. And with that ready, he charged again.

His intent was clear, murderous. One good swing to the side of the head with that stone would crush a man's head like an eggshell. His face grim now, Stumpy stepped to meet him. There was a whirling mix-up which was so fast that the watchers could not quite follow it, and out of it a bellow of pain. Then both men were standing still, Stumpy behind Bannack.

Stumpy's left arm encircled Bannack's neck, bending it back and painfully to the side, his grip all but shutting off Bannack's wind. His right hand had clamped on Bannack's wrist, twisting it back, so that with a little more pressure he could smash the bone like a pipestem. And as he applied the pressure relentlessly, Bannack's fingers opened, showing the stone, allowing it to drop to the ground.

For a moment longer, Stumpy held him. Then he released him suddenly, with a shove which sent Bannack sprawling in the dirt again. Stumpy turned to the staring nesters.

"Get him out of here," he ordered. "And if he comes back, I'll break his neck, next time."

They were a silent cavalcade as they rode away. Once, from a safe distance, Bannack turned to look back, a wild-eyed, terrible figure. But he voiced no threats.

"That was as pretty a lesson as I ever saw given tuh a bully," Chinook chuckled. Then he sobered. "But how about this other, Stumpy? Any chance of them makin' them charges stick?"

Stumpy scratched his head.

"Everybody makes a mistake, sooner or later," he said ambigiously. "And after what just happened to him—well, I sort of have a hunch that Bannack's about due to make his."

It had been the insult to Gloria, as much in tones as words, and the memory of past insults by this man, which had started him at Bannack. But he had pursued the humiliation with deliberate intent. Before the day was over, he knew that it was paying dividends. Shortly after noon, Chinook rode back on a lathered horse.

"Bannack's gatherin' a crew," he reported. "A big one—and they're startin' this way now, Stumpy. Aimin' to come in here and clean us out and take over by force, same as they did on the Wagon Wheel."

"I sort of figured, get him mad enough, that he'd not wait for the law to investigate us first," Stumpy nodded. "Only, at the Wagon Wheel and the Longhorn, the other side attacked first. This time, it'll be him who's doing that."

"Which puts him outside the law, this time," Chinook agreed. "And if he had any case, that spoils it."

"That spoils it," conceded Stumpy. "Providin' we win. All those other battles were stopped 'fore they hardly got well started. With this one, it'll be different. This is showdown—and just as much for Bannack as it is for us."

CHAPTER 22

STUMPY HAD a few uneasy moments as he considered his strategy. It wasn't fair to put it up to his men to kill and be killed, merely to insure him being in a position to win. It wasn't worth that.

But what might result from the fight had been an afterthought. He had lit into Bannack because of his insult to Gloria, and all the personal animosity which had been accumulating between them for months. Bannack had come to the ranch, had forced trouble, and had determined on revenge because he had been beaten. Whatever might be the results, the whole thing was inevitable.

Yet if Bannack did strike now, before the government men had any chance to investigate or make a ruling, that would put him in bad at the outset and strengthen Stumpy's case considerably. Which was a comfortable thought. Stumpy was being honest and above-board in what he was doing to get the land, and doing only what many another man in the west had already done. In doing it, he was paying his men good wages, as well as their keep.

Bannack was out to get land too, but he was trying to deceive honest homeseekers, paying them a bare living and no wages. If Stumpy won this battle, it would not be alone for himself and the Saddle, but for the nesters who had fallen under Bannack's power. For this, he recognized, would be a finish fight. When it was ended, one of them would remain in the country. Not both.

If Bannack lost, the nesters could get out from under his thumb and win the land they believed to be their own. The ironical thing about it all was that they were fighting now on Bannack's side, against the only man who could save them. Victory for Bannack meant defeat for them as surely as it could for Stumpy and the Saddle.

Stumpy had taken precautions. The big cattle herd was off in a valley where a couple of men could watch them, to prevent any stampede such as had been worked on the Longhorn. Now, if Bannack came for trouble, he'd have to meet the Saddle on their own terms. The buildings, like the scattered claim shacks, were reinforced with logs, built for bullets.

The weather, sunny a couple of hours before, had made a sudden change. A belated storm was sweeping out of the northwest, a mixture of snow and rain. Out of it came sweeping a ghostly line of horsemen, then more appeared from the opposite direction.

"We'll give them a warning shot," Stumpy said coolly. "Then, if they keep coming, give it to them."

There was no time for even this. A sudden chatter of

guns crackled from both ranks of the attackers, then bullets were whistling, splintering in the boards, thudding solidly in the logs. Chinook grunted and stared at a bullet-hole in his hat.

"Not bad shootin'—considerin'," he said. "And that hat set me back twenty bucks, just last week!"

The nesters were emulating Indians, sweeping away as soon as they had emptied their guns, and trying to pick moving targets in the storm was like slapping at fleas in the dark.

Without waste of time, the ghost riders were leaving their horses now, dropping off behind such shelter as offered, taking advantage of the storm to work up close on foot. The final end, if they could get close enough to fire the buildings, would be the same as it had been at the other ranches, for today Bannack had brought a crew which outnumbered the Saddle.

A lull had come in the gun-fire, but no one was fooled by it. Bannack had started something here that he had to finish.

The crew were taking the thing calmly, joking about it, though they all recognized the seriousness of the situation. Stumpy stood up.

"If we stay here and let them carry the fight to us, they'll get us, sooner or later," he pointed out. "And I don't care for that sort of thing. I want half of you boys to stay here and entertain 'em. The rest of us will get horses and go out to give them a real warm reception. They won't be countin' on that, and if we can get them on the run, we'll have things a little more comfortable."

There was an instant rush of men who wanted to go out, rather than remain in the buildings. Gloria came, wordlessly, her face white with anxiety.

"I'd like to go along, too," Gloria said. "But I can work a rifle from here as well as anybody."

"We'll need gun-fire to cover us, at the start," Stumpy agreed.

Five minutes later they swung the barn doors open and swept out suddenly, riding straight for where a group of the nesters had congregated in a clump of brush and boulders halfway up the slope beyond, from which vantage point, if not dislodged, they could be more annoying than a swarm of hornets overhead.

Sunshine was struggling to break through the clouds as they left the barn, the brief spring storm had ended. A horse went down under the smashing impact of lead, but the rest of them kept going, fanning out, holding their own fire until there was something to shoot at.

Someone set up a shout, mingled of surprise and dismay. Equally startled, Stumpy looked around and saw fresh horsemen heading toward them from the distance—six or seven riders, with badges glinting in the uncertain sun. One of them was Sheriff Cliff Vaughan. Others would probably be the federal marshal and deputies. Here again, as had happened on the Longhorn, the law had arrived in the middle of the storm.

For a moment, uncertainty gripped the invaders. Bannack had known that the law would be coming, to investigate the charges which he had filed, but in starting this all-out attack on the Saddle, it was plain that he had not expected them to get around for several days yet.

And by that time, he had aimed to have a case there could be no contesting—the Saddle in his own possession, the land automatically open to relocation because those who had taken it first would be gone.

The arrival of the law now was far from opportune, as regarded Bannack's plans. On what happened in the next few moments, much depended.

And then, panic gripping them, knowing that today they were fighting outside the law, some of Bannack's men made the same mistake as Cloud's had done before—swinging their rifle-fire on the newcomers.

Under that blast of lead, a deputy marshal slumped in the saddle, badly wounded. And the die had been cast.

Suddenly frenzied, the nesters stormed forward to the attack again, fighting with the desperation of men who see themselves caught in a trap. Under the bitter leaden hail sent at them, the charge of the cowboys faltered, broke, and Stumpy was forced to signal a retreat. As they turned, the depleted ranks of the lawmen joined them, moving back with them to the shelter of the buildings. Stumpy and Cliff Vaughan remained to cover them, keeping the retreat from turning into a rout, bringing back several wounded men.

They reached the shelter they had sallied out from so short

a time before, where the others, Gloria among them, cheeks flushed and hair disordered, were holding the nesters back with a withering fire. This slackened again, and they took grim stock of the situation.

"We were sent out here to investigate Bannack's charges against you, Stumpy," Vaughan said, slipping fresh shells into his revolver, regardless of a bullet furrow down his left arm. "But so far as I'm concerned, this gives you a clean bill of health—and you'll be needin' plenty of health, from the look of things. Meet Rusty Dolan, the Marshal."

Dolan, tall, square-built, with red hair and some of the same flame in his eyes, shook hands, jaw crag-like.

"I never knew such an outrageous happening before in my life," he protested. "What was their idea in the first place? To wipe you out before we could get here?"

"That seems to be it," Stumpy agreed. "It's Bannack's favorite method."

"So I've heard. But I'm surprised that nesters would fight the way they're doing. Ordinarily, they're a peaceful bunch."

"I think I can explain that," the sheriff suggested. "He's got most of them in a trap where they don't know what else to do, and he doesn't give them a chance to think. But the men who led them are like Bannack himself—gun-hawks. He's been importin' quite a few, this winter."

The marshal nodded grimly.

"That explains it. But Bannack will find he's picked a costly method, this time. I'll step out with a flag of truce and see if there are any clear-headed men that I can talk to."

"It's risky business, with Bannack headin' them up," Stumpy warned.

"They can't all be fools, not among the rank and file, and I don't want any more bloodshed," Dolan retorted. "If you'll cease firing and give me a chance, I'll have a try at it."

A moment later, opening the door, and carrying a white rag high on a pitchfork, he stepped out into the open, walking steadily forward for a hundred paces or so. The firing from the other side stopped as he advanced, the sun glinted on his red hair. Dolan lifted his voice so that it would carry for a mile.

"In the name of the law," he said. "I call upon all of you to throw down your arms. Then we'll talk things over."

There was a momentary silence, answered by Bannack's

voice, though Bannack remained hidden.

"And what'll happen when we talk things over?"

The marshal's answer was blunt, uncompromising.

"Everybody will be given a fair hearing. But those responsible for trouble, and murder, will be held to answer for it."

There was no answer, and he spoke again, impatiently.

"Don't you fellows see that you're in wrong, and getting in worse? You've no business in here, attacking this ranch. And when you fire on the law, it gets serious. Better show some sense."

"We'd like to talk it over a minute, among ourselves," Bannack called back.

"You can have five minutes." The marshal drew a heavy watch from his pocket, snapped it open and held it grimly.

Back with his men, Bannack was thinking fast. Dismay had struck him when he had seen the lawmen coming, arriving days in advance of what he had been led to expect. Trouble with the Saddle, with no outside witnesses, was one thing. The same sort of thing, with the law on hand to see, was a horse of a far different color. For Bannack knew only too well that the law had looked with considerable disfavor on his burning of the Longhorn, the previous fall.

Bannack's face grew bleak. He could hear his men talking excitedly among themselves, believing the fight was over, and glad of it. They were ready to quit, to sacrifice him to save themselves.

The five minutes was nearly up, the marshal still standing, rock-like, holding the flag of truce in one hand, his big watch in the other. Surrender now, after what had happened today, would almost surely mean the noose for Bannack. And in any case, it would mean victory for Stumpy Garford, an end to all Bannack's dreams of wealth and power. Kingship would be snatched from him, just as he had seen the crown within his grasp.

But if he went ahead as he had started! That was different. Most of his men had cold feet now and would like to quit. But if he shocked them to the point where it was a case of fight with him, or share the same responsibility, the same fate that stared him in the face if they lost—that again would be a horse of another color. A black horse with death in the saddle.

Bannack knew that his forces were overwhelmingly superior to the combined forces of the law and the Saddle. If the latter were wiped out—wiped out to the last man, so that there would remain no witnesses against them—

The marshal was snapping his watch shut. Deliberately, Bannack raised his rifle, pressed the trigger.

The white flag wavered, tumbled, while the echoes of the shot crashed like falling hopes. For a moment, Rusty Dolan stood rigidly. Then, blood gushing from a wound over his heart, the lawman pitched forward in his tracks.

CHAPTER 23

FOR A LONG moment, there was no other shot nor sound. Men on both sides were staring, appalled and shocked by the thing which they had just witnessed—the cold-blooded murder of a man under the protection of a flag of truce. Bannack swung on his own white-faced henchmen.

"That's that," he said. "We'll wipe 'em out—wipe them out to the last man—and woman! And when that's done, we'll have things all our own way, and no witnesses against us."

One of the bolder ones shook his head.

"You blasted fool!" he said softly. "What'd you want to go and do that for?"

Bannack levered a fresh shell into his rifle, impatiently.

"It was either that, or be run off this range," he retorted. "This way we win, the other we lose. There wasn't any choice—not after you fools fired on the law to start with."

"But if we do wipe 'em out—how can we ever explain such a massacre?" another man demanded.

"Easy. The Saddle fired on the lawmen, and we helped the law out. They put up a hell-to-breakfast battle as long as they lasted—and that's that. Snap out of it, you fools. We're all in this together now, and we've got to fight—or hang!"

He was giving them no time to think, to surrender him and disclaim his action. His dominant personality swept them again, making it seem logical enough, even to the most faint-hearted. More shots rattled out in a ragged volley, and the issue was decided.

For a moment, inside the shelter of the buildings, the lawmen and the cattlemen had been stunned by that wanton murder. But now, as the firing began again, they knew, as well as the others, that this would be a fight to the finish.

And within the next hour they recognized how grim that finish was apt to be. Bannack had his men where he wanted them now, where they dared not back out. Every shot which was fired made it more necessary to fire another. And they outnumbered the defenders more than two to one.

"The worst of it is, they'll keep creeping up on us till it gets dark, then some of them will manage to fire the buildings." Cliff Vaughan pointed out. "Once that happens and they burn us out into the open, with the firelight making targets of us, they'll just stay back beyond the rim of light and mow us down."

Stumpy recognized the accuracy of the sheriff's prediction. He had been prepared for a fight, but not for a battle of annihilation, such as this was developing back to. And the only thing that they could do was to fight back as well as they could, for as long as possible.

Escape was out of the question. That one charge had proven that an attempt to fight their way out wouldn't work. In the old days, one or two might have slipped out and gotten to the other ranches, or to Fortymile, for help. But now there was no help. The Saddle was the last ranch. Everywhere else, including Fortymile, were only more nesters.

And surrender was not to be thought of—not after what had happened to Rusty Dolan. Bannack didn't want any witnesses left, once this was done.

"Maybe we can make a charge, as soon as it gets dark," Vaughan suggested. "Before they can set any fires. That way, we can fight our way out—some of us."

"Best thing we can try, I guess," Stumpy conceded, and set about making preparations, while the rattle of gunfire continued without let-up. This would go down in the history of the valley as the last great clash between nesters and cattlemen.

But Bannack was making preparations for such a try at escape. Some of his men were gathering wood, and, keeping out of gun-fire, stacking it at intervals beyond. A try at escape would see these flares lit.

The sun was setting now, darkness was sliding down from the hills. Likewise, they had horses for not more than half the riders, and there were several wounded men who could not be moved.

Gloria came up beside Stumpy, her face colorless but composed as she looked briefly to the sunset.

"I'm going to stay here, Stumpy," she said steadily.

"I'm staying, too," Stumpy agreed. "Half of us will try and hold out, while Vaughan tries to get away and bring in help. As sheriff, he can deputize anybody he finds in town. If he makes it past their lines, they'll see how crazy it is to keep on fighting, and quit, likely."

He was speaking more confidently than he felt. With ordinary men, that would be true enough. But Bannack had a stranglehold of one sort or another over most of these homesteaders, and they had already fought to a point where now they believed that their only chance was to keep on, much as they hated it.

Vaughan came up, his left arm bandaged from the ripping thrust of a bullet, but smiling and holding out his other hand.

"I guess we'll be starting pretty soon, Stumpy," he said. "Here's luck—to all of us."

"That goes double," Stumpy agreed. "I—what's that?"

It was a fresh burst of gun-fire, but there was a new quality to it. It came from a distance, instead of close at hand, where the ring of steel had been closing in relentlessly during the last hours. Not quite drowned out by the guns were the wild hoops of fighting men.

There had been a momentary lull of the guns surrounding them. Now it broke out again, jerkily, but on one front, and the bullets were not drumming at them. Stumpy turned, running.

"It's help!" he jerked out. "Here's where we go out and take a hand!"

He reached a horse, swung to the saddle and was out through the door, the other horsemen hard on his heels. This time their charge was not checked. Something like panic had gripped the nesters at this unlooked-for change in the picture, for Bannack had assured them, as Stumpy had believed, that there was no one to help the trapped cattlemen. But the newcomers, whoever they were, were sweeping up like wolves to the kill.

Wolves! The panic among the nesters spread like wildfire. All at once it was over. Those who could do so had fled in the gathering darkness, and out of it galloped the wolf pack who had come in such timely fashion to the rescue, Wolf Masterson in the lead, a wild, gaunt figure with blood streaming from a wound in his shoulder, but still holding a smoking gun with his other hand. Behind him came the lawless legion who had been hiding with him in the hills during the long winter.

Masterson got down, a little unsteadily, but grinning as he looked around.

"Guess we got here in time," he said. "And I settled accounts with Bannack! He winged me, but where I sent him he'll cause no more trouble."

"Dad!" It was Gloria, and a moment later, careless of the blood, she was in his arms. Wolf Masterson held her close with his one good arm, a deep hunger in his seamed face.

"It's all right," he said huskily. "I've been a blind fool— and I reckon I'll have a lot to answer for, but since we got here in time, none of that matters."

Cliff Vaughan rode up and dismounted, a little wearily, from his horse. Masterson turned to him.

"Well, Sheriff, I reckon you'll be wantin' me," he said. "Here I am."

"How are you, Wolf?" Cliff Vaughan held out his hand. "Why should I be wantin' you? The only warrant against you was a federal one, and seein' that you've come to the rescue of federal men—well, I reckon this day's work will settle a lot of things, without rakin' up any more that needs to be forgotten."

Masterson stared, a little incredulously. He looked older, showing the ravages of the winter, and something of the imperiousness of old had been washed away in the winter's storms.

"Gosh, I—I wasn't countin' on nothing like that," he protested. "I've been a plain damned fool, though it took me a long time to find it out. Stumpy here, he's been the only man in the country to know where he was going and how to get there—"

"Looks like we're there now, Wolf," Stumpy said, as he came up. "Thanks to you. And we've got a nice herd of cattle here to keep going on with."

"Gosh, I—I'm hungry," Masterson blurted suddenly.

"Anything to eat around here?"

"Plenty." Gloria smiled and led him away, to where the cook was grumbling over the havoc that stray shells had done to his pots and pans. Presently she came back to Stumpy, and now she was smiling through a mist of tears. "Stumpy—"

Stumpy had no need to ask questions. He opened his arms, and she came into them with a little happy sigh, burying her face against his shoulder.

* * *

"Things aren't half as bad as I was afraid of," Cliff Vaughan reported. "For all the powder that's been burnt, there hasn't been much blood spilled—though what there was has been too much. But it will be a new country now, with the blight of Bannack gone. There will be no more contest of the Saddle, I can promise you that. And the federal men agree with me, that the best thing is to forget about what has happened, all around, and start with a clean slate for everybody."

"My idea exactly," Stumpy agreed. "Most of the homesteaders are honest, hard-working men, who didn't know what they were getting in to. Now they'll have a chance to go ahead and make homes for themselves, or at least have an honest try at it."

"Yeah, it'll be a decent country to live in," Vaughan agreed. He turned toward the door, swung back.

"By the way, you heard the latest news from Fortymile, Stumpy?"

"Don't know as I have. Anything interesting?"

"Sort of. Town's getting plumb civilized. Folks are startin' to build a church, and we've got a new sky pilot. Some man, too. Just thought maybe you and Gloria'd like to know."

This time he went out, and Gloria came in to the room. From the look in her eyes, Stumpy saw that she had heard.

"Reckon, if he keeps on, Cliff will rank as one of the major prophets," Stumpy nodded. "We'll have to have him for best man."

THE END